DANCES NAKED

Third book in The Fairies Saga

A Novel by
Dani Haviland

ISBN 978-0-9840308-0-4

by
Dani Haviland

~ The Fairies Saga ~
in chronological order

Naked in the Winter Wind

Aye, I am a Fairy

Dances Naked

The Great Big Fairy

Fairies Down Under

Preface

*F*airies, *Nûññë'hĩ the Cherokee called them, the Eternal Ones. They traveled to wherever they wanted without being seen. And, to whenever, too. They were invisible unless they wanted to be seen, were small—barely the height of a full-grown man's knee—and had long, black hair. They were friendly, and helpful, and, if you were nice to them, they'd be nice to you, and even bring you food. This crazy white man, Dances Naked, was all this, but he was easy to see, very tall, and had curly silver hair and a beard. He couldn't be a fairy. Or could he?*

Ж

20th century born Lord Martin Melbourne had received his master's degree from Oxford but was also well learned in folklore and the Tuatha De' Danann legends. He knew fairies weren't pastel-colored, exaggerated flying insects with big smiles–they were real entities with remarkable skills. They could move from one place to another easily–or from one time to another. He had studied The Letters, the centuries' old epistles written by the time traveler, Evie, to her 21st century daughter, Leah, and learned that a human, too, could move through time. He had done it himself, traveled back to 1781, and saved the life of his sons' ancestor. Now he wanted to go back home to 2013. But, he was lost in the wilds of North Carolina. He needed his new Cherokee friend to show him the way back to The Trees, the magnetic time portal between the centuries. But first, he'd have to wait until Red Shirt was done with him.

Ж

NAKED IN THE WINTER WIND, the first book in THE FAIRIES SAGA, tells the story of Dani Madigan, a plump and perky older Alaskan lady who takes a vacation to Greensboro,

North Carolina, to visit her daughter, Leah, a nurse. Through an accident involving the mysterious Master Simon, she falls through time on October 31, 2012 and awakens in 1780, without her memory and in a younger, thinner body. She rescues a mountain man, Ian Kincaid, who names her Evie and claims her as his wife. Months later, Ian takes her to visit his aunt, the time traveling fairy, Sarah Pomeroy, where he abandons her. Many events and people impact Evie's life, including the generous Little Bear and the evil British Captain, Atholl MacLeod, a rogue who shoots her in cold blood. Critically wounded, Evie is sent on an emergency medical trip back to the 21st century where she reencounters Leah. Moments later, Evie is kidnapped and taken back to the 18th century before she can explain to her daughter what has happened, where she has been the last year, and why she now has a youthful body. (Estimated release late 2012)

Ж

AYE, I AM A FAIRY continues the story with Leah finding clues about her mother's whereabouts in a misplaced cell phone. The reportedly gay James Melbourne, the British Lord her mother met the day she disappeared, contacts Leah. He has more information about her mother's disappearance in his bundle of ancient Letters. In the first of The Letters, Mom explains where she is, that the characters from *Lost*, the historical romance novels by Lisa Sinclaire, are real, and that some of these people are now her new family. Leah makes a new friend in James. The two suddenly have to ward off attacks by the numbered heirs of Atholl MacLeod, ne'er do wells who are searching for The Letters and the treasure they lead to. James receives another old letter, apparently from Marty Melbourne, asking him to go back in time to save his ancestor. However, it looks like he won't be traveling solo—Leah wants to go back, too. (Estimated release mid 2012)

Ж

THE GREAT BIG FAIRY introduces six foot seven inch tall Benji MacKay, an amiable soul born in the 18th century who returned with his parents to the 20th century as a child. Benji has read some of The Letters and heard about Evie. He searches out her 21st century daughter, Leah, meaning to travel back in time with her. However, he is too late. Life does not go as planned for The Great Big Fairy, but he makes the most out of what he has. He encounters and helps many people, including a six foot four female slave, in his journey back in time to see his beloved Grandpa Jody.

Ж

FAIRIES DOWN UNDER follows a certain member of the time traveling family who is transported on The First Fleet, the convict-laden ships sent from England to the newly discovered continent of Australia. He makes the best of his situation as he serves his sentence in the new, rough and tumble, no man's land used as a prison for convicts. (Estimated release 2013)

1 Strangers on the Road

Pomeroy's Place, North Carolina
August 12, 1781 late morning

Sarah Pomeroy watched the odd procession thread its way down the road. The scrawny, stringy-haired girl was overloaded with babies, one infant over her shoulder, the other in her belly. A dirty and disheveled man marched five steps ahead of her, his nose in the air, an overstuffed satchel slung over his shoulder. The mother didn't have anything other than her baby to carry, but Sarah remembered the fatigue and discomfort of an advanced pregnancy and sympathized with her. The woman-child shuffled behind the man then stopped, shifted the squalling baby to her other shoulder, then continued her trudge. The scruffy man halted, snorted indignantly, and waited for her to catch up. Well, almost catch up. As soon as she was five steps behind him, he picked up his long stride again, apparently not wanting her to be near him.

Sarah stepped away from her semi-secluded position in the tall weeds at the side of the road, waiting to be seen. She didn't want to frighten them or call out until they were near enough to converse. Maybe they had news about the war. The man looked up and saw her, but did not acknowledge her presence. He acted as if he had seen a crow or maybe a butterfly; she was a part of the fauna in the landscape and of no importance to him.

Well, to hell with him and his rudeness, too, Sarah thought. She would hear any news soon enough. Yes, but the young mother needed a break. If they stopped to speak with her, the woman could rest for a few moments at least.

"Hallo," Sarah hollered. The man looked up toward her. Well, actually he looked right through her, as if she didn't exist, and then continued his journey.

"I say, hallo," she repeated with an insistence that was hard to ignore. "Is there any news of the fighting?" she asked, now assuming a civil tone although, at this point, she wasn't feeling very cordial.

"Nope," he said without missing a step.

"Hold on there a minute," Sarah called out as she rushed over to them; it looked like the pregnant woman was ready to fall down. "Would you like to stop for a drink? I have some water here," she offered in desperation.

Sarah could tell by the man's stance that he was going to turn her down and that the swollen, downtrodden woman wasn't going to speak for herself. Sarah decided it was time to get bossy. "Hey, I think this woman needs a break," she declared. She changed her focus to the overheated young woman carrying the snot-faced baby. "Why don't you come sit a while in the shade and, here, I'll take the child," she said as she extracted the baby's fists from the mother's hair, not giving her a chance to refuse.

The very young woman, more a child than an adult, reluctantly relinquished her hold then stepped away from Sarah, not wanting to be familiar with her. She breathed a loud sigh of relief at losing her burden, arched her spine, and then rubbed her lower back with both hands.

The baby was not big; he was actually scrawny, and Sarah could tell why. The woman was most likely trying to nurse the child while in the advanced stages of pregnancy. Mother, youngster, and in utero infant were all suffering as a result. "Would you care to share my lunch?" she asked the girl, offering her a hand to help sit down in the shade.

The woman accepted the help and settled next to the maple tree. "If you're sure you have enough," she answered softly, allowing Sarah to see her smile of gratitude but still keeping her head bowed low, avoiding eye contact.

Sarah gave her a cheese-filled tortilla wrap sandwich, poured out a cup of water from her canteen, and then handed it to her. She sat down beside her new acquaintance and laid out the baby, placing it on the skirts of her dress. She took the kerchief out of her pocket, wet it with water from the canteen, and used it as a washcloth to wipe the baby's mucous matted face and eyes. The baby's clout was soaked and stinking, but she couldn't do anything about it here and now. She didn't have a dry one with her although there were plenty at the house. She briefly thought of inviting the little family to her home, but she knew she should find out more about them first. The woman seemed safe enough, but the man had an aura of evil about him that disturbed her.

"Where are you headed?" Sarah asked nonchalantly as she pulled the baby's sticky and sweaty gown away from her, or was it his, body; the child was covered in heat rash.

"None a yer business," boomed the man who had come over to investigate their little picnic site. Sarah had expected as much from him by his appearance, but it still took her by surprise when the rude words came out with such disdain. She turned to see the woman's reaction. Apparently, she didn't care what he said. All she cared about was eating the cheese burrito and gulping the last of the water in her cup, stealing glances at the canteen. Sarah took the hint and poured the woman's cup half full. She wanted to make sure she didn't give it all to her. It was a long walk home and the little bit of water in the jug was all she had.

The man remained standing over the two women, lording over them with the stance and tone he had taken. He brought out his own canteen, sneered at the women, and then started drinking heartily from it. Sarah doubted that it was water—it had the distinctive smell of raw alcohol.

"How about you—when are you due?" Sarah asked. Hopefully, the woman was just tired from the walk and not as dense as she appeared.

The only answer she gave was a shrug of her shoulders. She either didn't know or was afraid to answer. "Soon enough," the man answered for her. "Come on, let's go. There's no reason to laze about while the sun's still shinin'."

Sarah took pity on the woman as she struggled to get to her feet. She ignored her own better judgment and asked compulsively, "Would you two like to come to our place for dinner? You could sleep the night in the barn on clean straw and get a fresh start in the morning?"

The man looked as if he was getting ready to say no, so Sarah played her trump card. "We have meat," she said. "And fresh milk—it would be good for your wife."

The woman's eyes stole a look at the man then cut back to watching the ground. Sarah could tell she wanted to go, but he was a hard case. "I could pack you a little bit of food for the road tomorrow, too," she added, not wanting to beg but very concerned about the girl.

The man looked up toward the sun then down the road they still had to travel. "I guess we could take a break. We still have a couple a days to go and I could do with some meat. Do you have whisky?" he asked greedily.

Sarah didn't know how to answer that. The lure of having meat should have been enough of an enticement for the couple. She shook her head slowly then looked away, knowing he would be able to tell she was lying if he saw her face. "I think my husband traded the last of the whisky for some wheat." She turned to face him, "We do have some ale though," she added truthfully, letting him see she was being honest, at least with her last remark.

He sighed. "Lead the way then." He smiled to himself—maybe there were other things worth stopping for.

2 Rachel MacLeod

Near Pomeroy's Place
August 12, 1781 late morning

Sarah walked home with the ragged pair in tow. She had carried the baby for the first half mile, giving the young mother a break, until the man stepped in front of her and stopped, his feet planted firmly apart, his arms crossed in defiance. "Give the babe back to her," he growled. "It's hers to take care of."

Sarah didn't think it wise to challenge him so handed the now sleeping baby to the mother. The woman-child looked a little better for having the break but still appeared worn out. Hopefully, a hearty meal, a good night's sleep, and someone to help care for the baby for a few hours would help her further. She wished she could do more, but there was only so much an interfering bystander could do.

Prince Charles the jackass brayed to announce that someone was nearing the house. I saw a rag tag trio led by Sarah coming up the road. Apparently, she had rounded up a few strays, one of them very small, and brought them home to graze. "Here, let me take the baby," I suggested as I reached for the dirty and stinky bundle of rags. A red, pimply face poked out from beneath the threadbare cap, the eyes vacant and staring. The mother didn't like my gesture and clutched her child tighter, reluctant to relinquish her charge. She paused, shot a panicked look at Sarah, and then returned to her head bowed down position, emphasizing her fear and uncertainty.

"Let her take the child," Sarah gently admonished as she laid her hand on the young woman's shoulder. The disheveled and tired girl loosened her grip on the baby, lifted the mass of cloth away from her chest, and tentatively handed him or her to me. I led the way into the house and the two women followed, leaving the man to walk about the yard where he investigated the fence, then headed toward the barn.

Sarah guided the very pregnant girl to my chaise and helped her bring her feet up off the floor, lifting her tattered shoes to the foot of the couch, relieving the burden on her lower back and feet. I would guess that the girl, she could hardly be called a woman although she was very pregnant and the baby she was toting appeared to be hers, was only fifteen or so. And, I didn't know who stank worse: her or the child. Either way, I was glad there were two of us here to take care of the pathetic pair. They were definitely going to be a challenge.

Sarah helped the girl peel off her sweaty shawl. The stink almost made me heave. I grabbed the wooden tray next to the cupboard and used it as a makeshift fan to move the air. We didn't need me to add to the reek by losing my lunch.

"What's your name?" Sarah asked, both as a way to distract her from my impromptu air freshening antics as to make her, and us, more comfortable.

"They call me Rachel," she said softly, her head bowed down in apparent shame. Sarah looked over at me and raised one eyebrow. By the look of shock mixed with exasperation on her face, I could tell that even in the course of guiding the girl and the man on their long walk to the house, she had never seen the girl's eyes. Those four words were probably the first ones Sarah had heard her utter. Her body language was loud and clear though. She was a beaten woman; whether by whip or by words, it made no difference. She was a meek and totally subservient creature.

"I'm Evie and Sarah here is a healer," I offered as a further introduction and as an attempt to warm up the chilly atmosphere in the otherwise sweltering room. "Would you let her listen to your belly and see if the baby is okay?" I started to add that she didn't look too good and that we were both concerned about her, but bit back the words. They wouldn't have helped her or the situation anyway. I wasn't a doctor, nurse, or midwife, but her gray pallor could only be bad news. She gave the briefest of nods. Sarah moved in with her paper tube, her jaw set with concern. She too, could see what my untrained eyes had observed—a pregnancy in distress.

Sarah had everything under control so I decided to distract myself with the now sleeping child. His clothes were stuck to his body with his mother's sweat. I knew that very young babies didn't perspire and that was why his face was covered in the red pimply heat rash. I hated to waken a baby to change a dirty diaper, but this one was too rank not to take care of right away. Besides, it would only get ranker with time and the heat of the day. I looked around for something to place on top of the table before beginning the bath. I settled for my old blue patchwork skirt as a drop cloth. I spread it out, set the basin and towels on top of it, and then walked to the window to take one last deep breath of clean air. This was going to be tough.

The baby's cap was stuck on with a mixture of mother's milk, sweat, and baby vomit. I used a small, sopping wet cloth as a means of soaking off the cap from her/his head. I got a memory flash of the last time that I had to soak off disturbing fabric from someone's skull: Ian's bandage around his ears on the first day of our acquaintance. I shook my head and mumbled, "not now," and proceeded south with the disrobing.

Sarah looked up from her ministrations. I guess I'd been talking to myself louder than I thought. "It's nothing," I explained lamely, knowing that she would understand.

I unbound the layers of cloth on the child as I held my breath. I finally had to gasp. I couldn't leave the child and run back and forth to the window for fresh air like I was performing a task underwater. I knew I could get this done only if I breathed through my mouth. I opened my mouth, gulped air, and then realized the stench was so strong that I could actually taste it. I turned my head into my shoulder and breathed in my own body odor: warm, moist and musky but preferable to the baby poop and puke stench. I turned back to my task, once again holding my breath.

The baby woke up halfway through the unwrapping but just lay there, staring at the ceiling. I didn't know whether to be happy or sad that he or she was holding still and not kicking. I still needed to get the crap-encrusted diaper off in order to clean up the source of the stink. I pulled the clout away as gently as I could. Most of it came away with a squishy 'plop.' His legs just lay there: slack and leaden, his little penis bright red, and his balls huge. I knew baby boys' scrotums looked big in relationship to their bodies, but this was ridiculous. "Sarah," I called gently, trying not to show the panic I felt.

Sarah stood up straight from her bent over position. She had been listening with her improvised stethoscope for the heartbeat of the unborn baby in Rachel's belly. She didn't ask what, but she knew I needed her to see something. She followed my look and gasped. "Good God," she swore mildly. "Wipe the soft stuff off as best you can then soak his little bottom in the basin. I don't want you to rub, but let the water do the work on all the stuck on pieces of," she looked at me then ended her sentence with the silent, mouth-formed word, "shit." She shook her head then tipped her head toward Rachel who was reclined with eyes closed, letting me know wordlessly that her situation didn't look too good either.

Sarah sat back down at the girl's side but without the makeshift stethoscope. "When was the last time you felt the baby move?" she asked compassionately, as if this was her own daughter who was pregnant.

Rachel shrugged her shoulders then replied, "I don't know. I can't remember, but it was days ago." A tear was blazing a trail in the dust on her cheek. She knew the baby she carried was dead. "What do we do now?" she asked, her head tilted up, finally brave enough to look Sarah in the eye.

"Well, there are herbs I can brew that will get the uterus to expel its contents, but the pains will feel just the same as when you delivered your son here. It's still going to hurt, but Evie here knows a few tricks so it won't be quite so bad. Just let me know when you're ready, but I have to tell you, the sooner we get this done, the better your chance of survival."

Rachel's face skewed up as she listened. It was obvious she didn't understand Sarah's explanation. I translated it for her into plain and simple childspeak, "Sarah is going to give you a special tea so the baby will come out, but we have to do it right away or you could die."

"Oh," she said dejectedly but with total understanding. "Should I feed the boy first?"

I looked at Sarah and saw she wanted me to help. "I can do it," I offered willingly. "You're going to need all of your strength for the delivery." I looked over and saw the sweaty shawl in a heap on the floor. I didn't want to even touch it with my hands much less drape it across my shoulders as a scent diversion so the baby would nurse. Inspiration came to me with the sight of the stack of fresh clouts. "Just a minute," I said, "Sarah, watch that he doesn't roll off the table," even though we both knew he probably didn't have enough energy to move.

I rushed out to the well, refilled the ewer, and came back in. I held a clean clout over the basin and poured water over it. I approached Rachel with it and said, "Here, this is an old trick I learned a long time ago." I intended to use the cloth to wipe her face and neck in order to capture her aroma. She pulled back in shock at being bathed. I doubt that she did it herself much less let anyone else approach her is such a familiar manner. "I'm going to nurse your son but I need your body's, um, scent so he thinks that he's getting milk from you. I don't know if you saw them outside in the pen under the tree, but I have three babies I'm nursing right now so one more won't be a problem."

Rachel's eyes got huge. "Three?" she asked, "All at the same time? No, that couldn't be." She hung her head again and resumed her beaten down woman posture. "I'm sorry, I shouldn't talk so much."

"No, you're fine," Sarah declared. "But, I need to get the tea brewing. Evie, can you finish up here?" she asked as she cut her eyes over to the lethargic and still feces encrusted baby boy.

I tossed the clout with the eau d' Rachel over my shoulder then started soaking the boy's bottom. "What's his name?" I asked. I didn't want her to feel like she shouldn't speak, especially around other women.

"Atholl Grant MacLeod Junior," she replied, almost apologetically. "His father insisted the name be the same as his." She looked at Sarah, then me, and stuck out her chin in defiance, "But, I don't think he'll need to use the 'Junior' part of his name. I'm pretty sure his father is dead," she said then spat on the ground next to the bed, making both Sarah and me jump, "so he'll be the only one."

I squeezed my eyes shut, my hand still on Little Atholl's belly, and panted, trying to control the overwhelming urge to vomit. This was the son of the man who had robbed me, shot me, attacked Sarah and my little Jenny, killed her two biological brothers, and then was beaten to a bloody pulp by my husband after a grand confrontation involving Julian, Jody, Master Simon, and many Redcoat soldiers. If Captain Atholl 'Asshole' MacLeod was dead, and I was pretty sure that he was at least sentenced to die, I couldn't feel sorry for him. But, I really did feel compassion for his widow and son.

Sarah understood my shock and asked, "Then who's the other man? I thought he was your husband?"

10

Rachel shook her head quickly as if trying to erase the image of him being her husband. Maybe he had tried taking husbandly privileges and she didn't want his attentions, or maybe he was just a thug who she was with against her will. Either way, it was obvious that she didn't care for him. "He's my brother and," she started to say more but quickly bit her lip and repeated, "He's my brother."

Sarah went to the cabinet and took out her medicinal box. She rummaged through it and found the right little packets of herbs, took the smallest pot from the hook on the wall, nodded to excuse herself, and went outside to finish her task. The hearth fire was out—it was left cold in the summer. We cooked outdoors when the nights stayed warm. I craned my neck to look through the doorway, watching as she stoked the cooking fire. She brought the kettle to the well, filled it anew, and placed it on the hook of the iron framework above the flame.

I bundled up the baby boy who still stank but was as fresh as possible without more soaking. He couldn't help who his father was and I held him no animosity, but I couldn't bring myself to think of him as anything but 'baby boy.' I settled back on the porch bench, the damp cloth still draped over my shoulder, bared my breast, and urged the little tyke to nurse. He started fussing which I took as a good sign. A motionless baby is not a healthy baby unless he's asleep. This baby felt too warm and probably had a low-grade fever and I knew why. He had an infection in his little, well, not too little because of the swelling, male reproductive parts. We'd have to see what we could do about that later, but right now, he needed fluids. I pinched the skin on his arm and saw that it didn't fall back right away but stayed raised as a little ridge of flesh. Yes, he was definitely dehydrated.

His little mouth opened wide as if to cry but no sound came out, no tears. He gnawed on his fist and tossed his head back and forth. I didn't know if it was because I was not his mother or something else, but Rachel spoke up and explained. "He hasn't wanted to suckle for a few days now. I didn't know if it was because," she halted and looked down at her still swollen belly, "because the baby inside of me was dead or not. Maybe it made my milk bad."

I looked up at her as she held onto the doorframe, looking out at the playpen under the tree with my three healthy babies. They were all sound asleep at the same time, which was rare: I considered it a blessing taking into account the current situation. Sarah could use my help with this one.

Rachel was, or soon would be, a widow, and had a dead baby in her womb. Her one living child didn't look to be in such great shape either. She was still young and probably could have more children, but she already seemed worn out. "How old are you?" I asked noticing the look of amazement on her face when she saw that all three of my babies were the same size.

"Um," she halted, biting her bottom lip as if she didn't know if she should share the truth. "I'm fifteen come winter." She walked over to the playpen, holding onto the porch as she neared them. "These are all yours? And you had them all at the same time? And they all lived, or were there more?"

I shook the cloth with the eau de Rachel on it in front of the baby's face then replaced it just above my breast, but his face was turning toward his mother's voice. "Rachel, could you come over her and I'll tell you all about it. Your son is attracted to your voice so if you could talk over here next to me, maybe he'll nurse."

Rachel eased her way over to the bench beside me. I wafted the cloth again and answered, "Yes, all at the same time and there were only the three. They've all been very healthy, too; thank you, Lord. Are these your only two?" I asked, not only curious but wanting her to speak so the baby would hear her voice.

"No, the first one didn't make it. She was a girl and I thought she was fine but then, well, she died. Then I had him," she nodded to her son, "and then got pregnant again right away. I didn't know babies could come so close together."

Baby boy had started nursing when he heard his mother's voice. She grinned at the sight. "You seem to have lots of milk. I hardly had any the last few months. He tried real hard on the suckin' for a while but it hurt real bad, even made the nipples bleed, but there was hardly any left. And then, he stopped suckin' at all, so I tried givin' him some porritch and he did eat just a little. But, then my brother told me he was too little for it and I had to keep nursin'. He didn't want to believe me and got real mad when I said the milk was all gone."

Just then, Sarah came up with the brew. "It needs to steep for a bit longer, but I want you to get cleaned up a little and change your clothes." Sarah looked over at me and the baby. "It looks like your baby is nursing well. He'll be fine, I'm sure. After, um, uh," Sarah squeezed her eyes shut in thought. How could she phrase it without hurting the young mother's feelings?

I saved her from faltering in her explanation by interrupting her, which was either rude or gracious, depending on your point of view. "After," I continued, "you deliver this baby," I nodded to her belly, "you'll get more milk. As long as you get plenty of rest, food, and fluids, you'll have enough new milk to get him back on track, er, um, rather he'll grow to be a big, healthy boy. Now, do you have a home to go to, someone you can stay with after this is over?"

"We were on our way to a cousin's home in New Bern. He said he'd let me and the babies stay with him if I'd do the cookin' and cleanin'. My brother said he wasn't too happy about there bein' two babies, so maybe it's better that this one," she looked down at her swollen belly and said softly, "isn't going to make it."

"That is, was, not your decision to make," I asserted boldly. "Maybe God just wanted this baby up there with Him: did you ever think about that?"

"No," she sighed. She sat quietly thinking about what I had just said, then responded, "I think you're right though. Right now, God could take better care of him or her than I could." She started twitching in discomfort, as if the bench was covered in odd-sized pebbles. "How much longer? I want to get this over with." Rachel got up from the bench with the awkward difficulty of a very pregnant woman and limped back to the doorframe, leaning against it for support.

Sarah came close to speak with me. "I'd better get her set up. It's going to be a long night and I want to get a little something together for our supper before the real action begins. It looks like it's a good thing I didn't cut up both of those hospital gowns," she remarked. "She can wear the one while I get her clothes washed."

Just then, Wren woke up and let me know it was time for her supper. Jenny ran out from wherever it was she had been and picked her up, peeking down her clout to see how wet she was. "I got her for you, Mommy," she crowed. "Who's that?" she exclaimed at seeing me with a different baby. She did a double take, looking back to make sure her two brothers were still in the playpen.

"Oh, he's just visiting along with his mother and uncle. Now, Grannie is going to be very busy doctorin' tonight so you and Grandpa Jody and Daddy are probably going to be spending the evening outside or in the barn, okay?" I saw the sad look on her face. "And, I'll join you every chance I get, but I'm going to help Grannie. I'll need you to help with *all* of the babies though. Maybe this little boy can stay in the playpen with the others for a while. Would that be okay?"

"Three boys!" she shouted, bouncing around with Wren in her arms. "This family just keeps getting bigger and bigger and..."

I cut her off, "No, they're just visiting for a few days then they're going to go stay with their own family. Here, let me have

Wren. Would you go and tell your Daddy that I need to talk to him?"

I switched out babies, put Wren to my breast, and handed over Baby Boy to his eager, smiling mother. She really did love him even if she wasn't the most demonstrative woman in the world. I think she had just realized that there was hope for the two of them. I interrupted her reverie with an offer. "I'd like to get you all fixed up before we get started with the labor. Have you ever had the full salon treatment?"

She frowned at what must have sounded like a type of torture. I knew she didn't know what I was talking about, but I didn't want to be in close quarters with a laboring woman who hadn't bathed in Lord only knows how long. "Just trust me, okay? It'll just be us; all you have to do is sit or maybe stand a little." I looked around for my number one helper but didn't see her anywhere. Her radar was keen though so I just called out, "Jenny, would you get me my little wash basin and bar of sweet smelling soap, please?"

"Okay, Mommy," she shouted from behind the house somewhere. Seconds later, a green calico flash streaked past us and quickly reappeared with a bundle. "I brought the pink towels, too. Do you want me to heat some water for you? I can do that. Are you going to wash her hair? I'll go get the comb and brush if you want me to."

Jenny was spouting off her suggestions rapid fire like always. Rachel smiled softly at her. I could practically see her visualizing the daughter she had lost when she looked at her. "Yes, dear, that would be fine," I answered. At least it didn't look like I was going to meet the resistance that I had feared. From the way Rachel had pulled away from me earlier when I wiped her face, I thought that I'd have to resort to strong-armed means for the bathing.

Sarah briefly joined our party, bringing with her a cup and a little pot with the labor-inducing brew. "Now this isn't going to taste very good. I put some honey in it, but I'm not sure that will help. I want you to drink it all within the next ten minutes. Come back in the house for more instructions when you've finished getting cleaned up."

Sarah saw the frown furrowing the young woman's brow and offered the only comfort she could. "This um, delivery was going to happen with or without our assistance. At least this way you're not going through it by yourself and your other baby's needs will be seen to. He has an infection but if you keep his bottom clean, that will probably take care of the rash. Now, let Evie pamper you and then, when you've got this gown on, come on inside."

Rachel pulled her lips taut and tried to smile but only managed a grimace. What a time to be selected as queen for a day! She had never received so much attention in her life. Now these women were being nice to her and it was for the gruesome event of the birth of her dead baby.

While Sarah gave her instructions, I multitasked, nursing my daughter, and moving bits and pieces to clear an area for us. I set up our little day spa on the side of the house so it was out of view of the road and the barn. The newly washed quilts were still on the line and afforded us extra privacy. I brought out a kitchen chair and Jenny toted water. I returned Wren to the box of baby boys and began my Queen of Clean chore. I started at the top of Rachel's head, shampooing her hair twice to cut through the built up oil and crud. After her hair was clean, she relaxed. Jenny busied herself scrubbing feet while I did the best I could with a sponge bath, letting her cover herself with bits of cloth as I worked my way from her neck down to her ankles where I ran into Jenny's domain.

"Could you stand up so I can get the back of you?" I asked.

Rachel looked down at Jenny then over at me. "Can she leave for just a bit? I think I heard my baby cry," she said softly.

"Jenny, you heard her—please leave us alone for a few minutes, okay?"

Jenny opened her mouth to protest. We all knew that no baby had cried. But, my sweet little girl saw the look in my eye and obeyed without complaining. "Yes, Mommy, but I'll be real close if you need me."

"Yes, dear, that'll be fine," I said then turned back to my task. Rachel stood up slowly, grabbing the back of the chair to steady herself. She turned around and presented her back to me, the pink towel clutched to her chest. I let out an unintentional gasp. She was scarred from her shoulders to her buttocks. She had been whipped repeatedly, and the scars were in various stages of fading. My eyes went lower and then I couldn't help but proclaim, "Dear Lord." She had fresh, red slashes on the back of her legs. Someone had whipped her in the last day or two. "Why?" escaped my lips as I wet the rag and gently started washing her back and shoulders.

"I wasn't moving fast enough, at least that's why he whipped my legs. He said it was the only place he could get to that wouldn't ruin my dress. He couldn't punch my face like he used to. He was afraid that someone would come up and see me."

I'm sure that she saw the horror in my face. But, instead of clamming up like she would have done earlier, she grinned, happy to have someone to tell the story to. "You see, that's what happened a long time ago, when I was a couple years younger than Jenny. A fur trapper had just come up to the house to see if we had any cornmeal to trade. He was a pretty, white man but dressed like an Indian. He saw my face all red and puffy and asked what happened. I wouldn't tell him, but then he heard Grant tell me to shut up when he asked me about it. Well, the trapper sent me inside to pack up some of the cornmeal and then I heard the fussin' out by the barn. He beat the tar right out of Grant. Well, not exactly tar, but close enough." Rachel was grinning with the memory. "Yup, Grant never beat me in the face again. It's a good thing, too, or I wouldn't have any teeth left. See, he knocked that one out," Rachel said as she opened her mouth and showed me where a bottom tooth was missing.

I gulped, nodded, and hurriedly finished her sponge bath. Evidently, Sarah had poured a healthy dose of whisky into the tea; I could smell it on Rachel's breath. Rather than try to comb or brush her hair though, I let her run her fingers through the first layer of snarls and tangles. It was too much of a challenge for me right now. If she had been my daughter, I would have cut it all off and let it grow out again. But, long hair was the standard in this era and a short haircut would have been an insult to her character.

As it was, her coif was a non-issue; what I cared about was her smell and hygiene. She was clean now and didn't stink—well, not much. There was still the lingering smell of something dead around her. We all smelled it; I could tell by the sniff, sniffs that all of us had done before we realized what it was. But, no one said anything. Jenny had started to make a remark earlier, but I quickly distracted her with a chore. "Would you please take care of the babies? I didn't get a good burp out of Wren or, um, the new baby boy."

"Okay," she said very willingly. "But, what's the baby boy's name? It can't be Baby Boy, can it? Hey, can I give him another name? He can have two names, one for when he's at home, and one for when he's here. Huh, can I?" she begged.

"Absolutely!" I declared. Now, she was both distracted from the source of the stink, and could come up with another name for the boy. Any name would be better than the one his, ugh, father had given him.

3 The Unwelcome Stranger

Pomeroy's Place,
August 12, 1781 early afternoon

Wallace decided to call the job done—he had whacked enough weeds for the day. He walked in from the back of the garden, admiring its progress as he approached the house. A smug grin of satisfaction settled on his face as he replaced the hoe into the tool rack. He had to set a good example for Jenny. She was easily distracted and tended to go from one task to another before cleaning up after herself. He had moved the tool rack down two feet lower just so she could reach it without a stool. It was hard to believe that she had been in their lives for less than two weeks. She had fit in with all of them from the very beginning, the thumb in the glove of his family.

Suddenly he heard an unfamiliar sound. It was a man coughing—a hoarse, rattling cough that ended with a wet sounding discharge. He looked over at the source of the noise. Next to the barn was a gangly stranger, his hands busy as he walked along the north wall, picking up the nesting boxes, peering under and around each one, and then setting it back down. The raggedy man was unknown to him and was being a bit too familiar with his investigation of the Pomeroy property. Neighbors and travelers always approached the house and announced themselves before going to the barn. He tried his best not to judge a person, ever, but especially not before speaking with him. But, he didn't like this man. There was something sinister and uncomfortable about him.

Wallace walked toward the barn and the stranger. He looked back toward the house to verify that his little family was safe. He saw Jenny holding Wren and Evie with another baby. What? That wasn't his child—it was too big. Or rather, it was too long. His babies were shorter but nice and round and filled out. This one was scrawny and had a very red face. Oh, there she was—the other mother. A sad faced young woman, very pregnant and obviously tired, was leaning against the doorway. Sarah was tending to the kitchen fire. By the scowl on her face, it looked she was getting ready to get busy. The snooping man must be part of that little family. Regardless whether or not he liked the looks of the man and his nosy attitude, his own sense of propriety dictated that an introduction was in order.

Wallace walked over to the man who was now inside the barn, lifting a coil of rope off the wooden peg. He stuck out his hand and introduced himself, "Hello, I'm Wallace Pomeroy-Hart. May I help you?"

The scruffy man looked down at the offered hand then back up at Wallace. "Do you live here?" he asked, foregoing the handshake and ignoring the question.

Wallace brought his hand back to his side, surreptitiously wiping his palm on his pants. The proximity of the man made him feel dirty. But, Wallace wasn't a small man in any respect. He would turn the other cheek at the man's snub. He pulled himself up to his full six foot five inch height and answered the man. "This place belongs to my father and his family. I live here as does my wife, four children, father, and mother-in-law. What business do you have here, sir?"

The man looked up at Wallace, squinted one eye and snorted, "Hmph," then walked outside, once again dismissing Wallace's question by ignoring it.

The man's attitude was one Wallace had never encountered. It was more than rude and beyond disrespectful. And, this man obviously didn't have an ounce of courtesy or respect for another person's property, either. Now he was walking over to the grain storage shack. "Excuse me, sir," he called after the nameless stranger. "There's nothing in there for you."

"Maybe there is and maybe there isn't," sneered the man. He grabbed the crossbar and jerked on it, trying to pull it out of its brackets. Wallace leaned back against the fence post and grinned. The man didn't know about the locking pins, hidden on the bottom of the supports. No Name spat on his hands and tried again, grunting and sweating more and more with each attempt. Wallace sighed loudly, but didn't say anything. "Well, it's the wrong time of year for the whisky anyway," the man said as he turned away from the locked door, admitting defeat with his sour grapes explanation.

Wallace walked behind Mr. Rudeness as he headed toward Sarah and the fire pit. The stranger stood right in front of her and demanded without preamble, "Where's the meat you promised?"

Sarah lifted her arm and wiped her brow with the back of her wrist. Wallace could see that she was trying hard not to lose her temper—she was biting her bottom lip as she composed her thoughts. When she realized Wallace had walked up to join the conversation, she relaxed her clench. Her son-in-law nodded to her that he could handle the situation, so she let him do the talking. "We'll be having meat on the spit this evening. You and your family are welcome to join us, Mr…"

The stranger turned sharply and glared at Wallace then turned his attention back to Sarah. "You didn't say we'd have to wait for nightfall. Give me the food for the road then, and we'll leave right now. We have a long ways to go."

Sarah inhaled deeply which, rather than having the calming effect of composure, seemed to fuel her fire of impatience. She wasn't going to let this man intimidate her, even if he was a master of that black art. She had Wallace here for protection if the scum did decide to get physical, although he seemed the type who worked with words only. "Your sister won't be able to go anywhere for a few days," she said through clenched teeth. "She's going to deliver the baby tonight. If you want to eat, you'll just have to wait a bit longer. I can offer you bread and ale for now, but the meat will be a few hours more."

Sarah looked up and behind the man to Wallace. He once again gave a slight nod. She didn't have to tell him what was going on. He knew childbirthing was neither a quick nor an easy task. He looked at her again to make sure she understood that yes, he would tend to the meat for dinner and anything else that was needed.

"Where's the whisky?" the man demanded. "You said there'd be whisky."

"I, I did not!" Sarah blurted out with exasperation. "I told you we had ale. Wallace," Sarah was biting her bottom lip again, trying to contain her steadily increasing rage at the man's rudeness, "would you get mister...what *is* your name?" she demanded. He wasn't going to get anything else until she at least knew his name.

"Mr. Grant MacLeod, if you really need to know, which you don't," he said as he looked up toward the sun, apparently trying to gauge the time of day.

Sarah and Wallace looked at each other quickly then broke eye contact. Sarah bent back down to the kettle with the muslin bags of black cohosh root, juniper berries, slippery elm, and rue. Wallace looked over at Evie, making sure she was okay. Did she know who this man was, or at least his family name? Yes, she probably did. She was frowning and staring down the road to the mill, rubbing her left shoulder, the shoulder where she had been shot less than two weeks ago by that worthless excuse for a man, Captain Atholl MacLeod. Wallace looked back to the pregnant woman. He saw her gaze at his children in the playpen, a slight smile trying to crack her stone countenance. Then she put her hand on the top of her swollen belly and the chance at happiness glow was gone, a hard, angry look replacing it.

"Well, where's the ale?" groused Grant. "I'm thirsty!"

Wallace shifted his eyes over to the ungrateful guest. Something was very wrong with this scenario, but he would have to wait to find out more. He wasn't going to speak with Sarah or Evie about it until this man was out of hearing range. "Why don't you go sit down under that tree in the shade? I'll bring you a bottle of ale and a bit of bread. Would that suit you?" Wallace asked with only a slight hint of disgust.

"Better make that three bottles—I don't want you havin' to run back and forth all the time," he replied, ending his comment with sinister laugh that made both Sarah and Wallace shudder.

"How did you wind up with him?" Wallace asked Sarah as they headed to the springhouse.

"Lord only knows," she replied sharply. She looked over at the practically catatonic mother who would have to deliver a dead baby later. "Yes, the Lord does know," she said, this time with determination. "And I'll do my best to save the mother. The baby's already dead." Wallace's eyes widened with shock. "Oh, I'm sorry, you didn't know. The baby has been dead for a few days. We have to get it out before she dies, too. Her other child is in rough shape but can bounce back with good care. Wallace, the baby is Atholl MacLeod, Jr. The woman is Rachael and she said that, that 'Grant' is her brother. Do you think...?"

"Hey, where's the ale?" hollered Grant. He had pulled a quilt off the clothesline and was wadding it up to use as a pillow.

Wallace gritted his teeth. He swallowed his rising anger and counted to ten in Latin before he spoke. "I'll be right there," he called back. He put his hand on Sarah's shoulder. "I'll get back to you on that," he said softly, then headed to the springhouse for the ale.

I had heard the shouting about ale and realized that the brother would probably want something to eat, too. Hopefully, he was the type who would eat and drink then fall asleep. Well, we didn't have that much ale so that wasn't likely. I looked over at the covert stash of painkillers that I had brought back with me from the 21st century. Nope, I'd better not. It would be too easy to slip a ground up Percocet into a sandwich with hopes that the creep would fall and stay asleep until the birthing was over.

"Wallace, I'll make our guest something to eat," I called out. He waved his hand in acknowledgment.

"Sorry 'bout this, Lord" I said softly as I looked skyward. "I'm just conserving our provisions and helping the man get a good nap."

Hey, what can I say? Sometimes we decide to take the easy way out. I had four babies and a pregnant woman I was going to have to contend with this evening. I'd rather have Wallace helping Sarah and me than kowtowing to a belligerent sot.

I scraped off as much ham as I could from the bone that I had held back for the pot of beans. I combined the meat and two pulverized pills into some grated cheese, fought back the impulse to spit into the mix, and then smashed the works into a heel of bread, making a little ham and cheese pasty for the greedy man. This would have to do him until supper, if he was even awake by then.

I looked over and saw Jenny was with the babies and Rachel was seated on the porch bench again. She really was pathetic but I could only help her body right now. The mind healing would take longer and would probably involve Divine intervention. "I'll be right back, Jenny."

"Can I have some, Mommy?" she asked when she saw the sandwich.

"Not this one; I'll make you one when I get back. Why don't you get our lady guest a drink of milk?"

"Okay," she answered, then quickly jumped up and ran to the barn, eager to help. Rachel sighed as she watched my little girl, happy and healthy, bound across the yard in front of her.

"Your son will be healthy soon, too," I remarked. "And you can eat solid food after we get the, after the delivery." I gulped at the awkwardness of the remark then returned to the task of serving the grump his snack.

"Well, what took you so long?" he asked with an insincere smile and a stare that took me aback. Oh, God—it wasn't a smile—it was a leer!

"Here, enjoy it," I said as I dropped the plate in his lap and left in a hurry, almost running. I didn't care if I had made a mess or not. If he was hungry, he'd eat it. I wasn't going back to within three yards of him again without an escort, an armed escort. He may be just the brother-in-law of that asshole Captain MacLeod, but he gave me the same creepy, crawly feelings.

Wallace ran to catch up with me as I scurried to the house. "Hold on," he said as he pulled me away from the porch steps, away from Rachel and Jenny who were sharing a big mug of milk. "What's going on?" he asked.

"That, that…creep! God! Are you sure he's only Rachel's brother? He, he, he leered at me just like Asshole!" I was wiping my arms with my hands, trying to erase the feeling of insects crawling all over me.

"Her name's Rachel?" he asked, "Rachel MacLeod?"

"I guess. I mean, I know her name is Rachel, and her baby is Atholl Grant MacLeod, Jr., but I don't know if she is, or was, married to *him*. I didn't ask, but that seems to be the usual way of doing things around here, I mean *now*, shoot, you know what I mean!"

I was getting exasperated and he knew it. He put his arm around me and held me tight despite the heat. I didn't care either—I hugged him back even tighter. "It's going to be okay," he said. "It has to," he added as he let me go. "But I have to tell you. The man's name is Grant MacLeod."

"What?" I exclaimed too loudly. I looked over and saw Jenny and Rachel looking over at us. "It's okay," I lied to the women. "What?" I repeated to Wallace, softly this time but with just as much curiosity and amazement.

"Well, it looks like the three of them are siblings. At least that's the only way I can see that Rachel and Grant are siblings and the baby is, um, 'A.M.' junior. Lord, how old is she? She looks like a child."

"She's only fourteen and this is her third baby. I don't think I want to know what happened to the first one. But, I do know that we're here to help her with this third one and also the second one. He has an infection, but I'm sure cleaning him up and keeping him that way will help. Rachel will get milk again after she delivers this baby, the dead part doesn't make a difference, and then she can bring the boy back up to speed."

"Huh?" Wallace asked, not recognizing the 21st century slang that I had lapsed into.

"I mean, he'll catch up on growth and weight gain with nursing if she eats right and gets rest. She was on her way to live with a relative in New Bern when Sarah saw them on the road. Hopefully, she'll get rid of Grant along the way. Please, don't leave me alone with him, not even for a second." I realized that I was subconsciously rubbing my still tender left shoulder as I asked, rather begged. Time may heal all wounds, but there hadn't been nearly enough time for the emotional and physical wounds of being intentionally shot by a lecherous child molester to even scab over my injuries.

4 Delivery

"So, what do we do now?" Rachel asked glumly. "I want it to be over with. Ooh," she groaned as she suddenly grabbed her stomach and leaned forward. "I think it's starting. My belly hurts now."

Sarah cut a glance over to me, a trace of fear in her eyes. I doubt that the tea had had a chance to work yet. That meant either Rachel was losing the baby on her own or there were complications. The words 'detached placenta' flashed into my mind. I reached out and grabbed Sarah's hand with my right and Rachel's with my left. "Lord, please help us in this, this procedure. We know you have the baby with you now, but please keep Rachel safe here on earth. She has the other baby to see to still. Thank you in advance for taking care of all our needs; in Jesus name, Amen."

I breathed a deep sigh of relief. "There, now I feel better. Everything's going to be fine." I turned to Sarah. "Excuse me, but if you don't need me, Sarah, I'll go get dinner started."

"Thanks. Go ahead—I'm fine for now. Rachel, would you lie down here, please. Let's see what's going on." She patted and prodded her patient and talked softly to her as I gathered up the plates and utensils to take outside. I didn't want to get too close to the woman emotionally. I already felt like I knew too much about her and her perverted brother.

I got dinner under way and came back to talk to Sarah. Something was bothering me and I had to share it. I pulled her outside and asked discreetly, "Do you think that a little whisky might be a good idea? Not so much for the pain but for the shock of the, well, you know." I didn't want to say that it would be so Rachel didn't freak out when she saw her dead baby, but Sarah knew what I meant and obviously agreed.

"I put a bit in the tea, but you're right—it might soften the blow." She went back inside and pulled out a half-full bottle of whisky from under the cupboard. "I don't think we should cut it with honey and milk," she told me. "The more we get into her in the next hour, the better. She's progressing rapidly. Normally I wouldn't want a labor to go this quickly—it's hard on the baby—but in this case, it doesn't make a difference."

"If that's whisky, can I have some?" Rachel asked when Sarah stopped talking. "I want to be blind drunk when this baby comes out. You'll take care of the body, won't you? I don't want to see it."

Rachel had been reclining when Sarah brought out the whisky, but elbowed her way up to a sitting position with the offer of oblivion. "If there's ever any whisky around, Grant gets it. Ooh, there's another one," she winced as she grabbed her lower belly.

She started huffing and blowing without instruction. I watched as she finished her contraction with a cleansing breath, just like I would have told her to do. It appeared she was already employing the Lamaze method. "Where did you learn to do that?" I asked. "I mean the breathing during the contractions."

She shrugged her shoulders. "When I was pregnant with the first baby, my daughter, I didn't know what to do, how to birth the baby. Our mother was dead, and I didn't know anyone else that could help. My brothers didn't know or care about how babies came out. 'Hey,' they said, 'the cat can have kittens without any help so you can, too.' So when it was her time, I went out to the barn and watched the cat have her kittens. I saw that she did the breathin' when her tummy got hard and, well, she did yowl right there toward the end when the first one came out, but after that, she was okay. So, I just did the breathin' when little Esther started to come. But, I didn't yowl or holler or nothin', ever! My brothers knew what was gonna happen and said I'd probably scream 'til my throat bled, but I didn't. I wasn't gonna let them have the satisfaction of hearin' me hurtin'. It was all their fault anyway."

I was stunned and didn't know what to say. Wallace had told me he thought that this baby was the result of incest, that she was little sister to both Grant and Captain Asshole. So, rather than ask about why it would be their fault, I decided to ignore the remark and offer my help as a coach instead. She was doing fine by herself, but since I was already here, I might as well make myself useful. I put one hand on her belly and said, "Here, let me hold your hand and, oops, here's one now. Start your breathing."

Well, every couple of contractions merited a drink and she wasn't just sipping the firewater either. She was handling her labor better than I had, although I knew her pains had to be just as intense. Of course, by now, I doubt she was feeling any pain. I was surprised she was still awake.

"I didn't want to do it so that's why he gave me the whisky the first time," Rachel said, her eyes glazed. It was if she was reliving that moment. She tossed back another shot. "Atholl told me to drink some of it, that it would make me feel real good and warm inside. It smelled nasty and I didn't want it, but Grant glared at me, picked up a branch and started whittlin' the little side shoots off of it, so I gulped it down. Atholl started rubbin' up against me, his hands all up and down my chest and backside, and then he grabbed me and started kissin' on me and pullin' at my dress. I was only eleven and didn't know what was going on but did know I didn't want to take off my clothes. It was winter and cold and we only had a small fire. But, he hit me and said he'd beat me good if I didn't take them off, that he'd cut the dress off me and maybe take a little skin, too, if I didn't do as he said."

Rachel was still staring off into space, replaying the episode of shame in her mind, but not sharing the gory details. She put out her little cup and Sarah added a healthy shot of amber anesthesia to it. A contraction hit suddenly, I squeezed her hand, and she transitioned into labor breathing mode, forgetting everything else. The contraction ended and she turned to stone, only her slow, steady breathing indicating that she was alive.

The air had become heavy with the awkward silence and, evidently, Sarah felt it, too. I could see her twitching, fidgeting with her skirts.

Rachel started speaking again just as suddenly as she had stopped. "So I could do it with or without the beatin'. And Grant: he just sat there and watched, never sayin' a word, just holdin' that switch, smackin' his hand with it, checkin' it out to make sure it was nice and smooth. He was hopin' I wouldn't do as I was told so he could hit me. You see, Atholl didn't let him beat me unless I had been bad. Those two didn't really get along or care much for each other..."

I squeezed her hand again; the contractions were coming much faster now. Rachel stopped talking and started her huffing and puffing again. Her eyes widened and then she started panting. "Phew, that was a big one," she said after the contraction ended. "Anyhow, Atholl was bigger and older than Grant. He used to call him names and make him feel bad. I think that there's somethin' wrong with Grant, I mean because of the names that Atholl called him, but I really shouldn't talk about it; it's real personal. But, it's just as well I suppose, because he never bothered me 'that way', still doesn't. But he sure gets mean sometimes."

Rachel tipped back the last of the whisky in her glass and then set it down awkwardly. She was definitely drunk now. "So, late the next summer, I had Esther. She was beautiful and didn't cry too much. I saw that the animals got milk after havin' babies and I did, too. She was real easy to take care of..." Rachel felt me squeeze her hand and started her breathing. She exhaled after it was over and said, "They're getting' real close together now, I think, and tougher, too!"

"So anyway," she continued her story like the labor she was enduring was a minor inconvenience to her story telling. The liquor was certainly loosening her lips. "I had to take care of the animals and the baby. It wasn't a problem though because we only had a few chickens and a couple of goats. I had been outside for a little bit longer than usual because I wanted to get all the eggs. We didn't have a hen house so I had to go lookin' in the bushes and where all for the eggs. Esther was asleep when I left. She was still quiet when I got back so I didn't pay her no mind. I cooked the eggs for Atholl and me for dinner. Grant wasn't home; I can't remember…" I squeezed Rachel's hand and she was huffing and puffing right away.

"I gotta get this out!" she exclaimed in exasperation.

"Let me check you," Sarah said in her midwife tone, "It might be time…"

"No, no," Rachel screamed. "Not the baby. I have to tell someone! It was Atholl! He killed my daughter, his daughter! She wasn't sleeping when I checked on her—she was dead. He had pulled off her clout, and she was all bloody down there, and she was dead! Aaahhhhh!"

I could tell by Rachel's belly that she was contracting, but I don't think the soul-shaking scream was from that. Still, I rushed down to her feet and applied my thumbs to the pressure points on her soles, trying to ease, at least, her physical pain. There wasn't anything I could do for her mental anguish. I doubt any amount of alcohol could numb that pain.

"He killed her and it was all my fault. I told him to leave me alone, that I didn't want to do that no more. I, I, should have let him…Aaaaahhh!" Another contraction and another scream so powerful, it seemed to rattle the teacups on the counter. It was either from anger, frustration, or pain, but most likely from all three of them. This young girl had definitely been through a lot.

Sarah sat down at the foot of the chaise and pushed apart Rachel's knees, stuck one hand on the distended belly and the other up inside of her to check her dilation.

"It's time for her to push," Sarah told me. "Get behind her and support her shoulders. I don't know how much help she's going to be though; she's pretty snockered."

So, I stood behind Rachel and Sarah pressed on her belly and yelled 'push.' It must have been good instincts because Rachel was so drunk she couldn't sit up by herself but still gave a couple of hearty pushes until Sarah hollered, "Whoa, stop pushing!"

The smell hit the air even stronger than when her water broke earlier. But, we all—well Sarah and I—were high on adrenaline and the odor didn't bother us a bit. "It was the cord," she said softly to me as she unwrapped the cord from around the baby's neck. "Now push again," she ordered Rachel.

Rachel obliged and two seconds later a perfectly formed, but dead and gray, baby girl was born. She was about the same size as Wren had been when she was born which meant she was probably four to six weeks premature.

Sarah wiped the baby's vernix off and wrapped her in a cloth. "Here," she said to Rachel. "You have to see her. She's perfect. The umbilical cord was wrapped around her neck. There wasn't anything you or anyone else did wrong, and there was nothing anyone could have done to save her. Look at her. She's beautiful."

Rachel was immediately alert and sober, or at least appeared to be. She rolled over on to her side and held the bundle that Sarah placed next to her. "Look," Rachel said softly and tenderly, "she has hair already. And you're right—she is beautiful."

Rachel started to cry silently and let the tears fall for a full five minutes before she attempted to rein in her emotions. She sniffed and wiped her nose and eyes on the shoulder of the hospital gown. "So it wasn't my fault that she died?" she asked.

"Not your fault or anyone else's." Sarah said emphatically. "And everything went well with this delivery so you can have more babies. That is, after you find a good man and remarry. I'm sure there are many men out there who would love to have a wife as lovely as you with a ready-made family. At least he'd get a son right off the bat!"

Rachel smiled at the remark. "Thanks for making me look at her. It does help. Should I give her a name?"

Sarah nodded rapidly. She had named her stillborn daughter years ago and I'm sure she was glad she did. Rachel looked over at me for my opinion.

"You can name her whatever you'd like. She is *your* daughter," I encouraged. "You knew her before she was born, when she turned over inside of you, kicked you in the ribs. She is, and always has been, yours. And, now she is with the Lord." I hoped I was saying the right words. They came from my heart and not from experience.

I still had amnesia for the most part. My short-term memory was fine. I clearly remembered the last twelve months and the births of my triplets, but remembered nothing of Leah, my first born from my previous life in the 20th and 21st centuries, until I came face to face with her.

Leah had been my recovery room nurse a week ago chronologically calculated, but 232 years into the future according to the calendars. Although I had no recall of, well, anything of my previous life in the 21st century, I knew that I was her mother the moment I saw her, the obvious age discrepancy not even a consideration. I guess the maternal bond was stronger than the chemicals or whatever it was, that had erased my memory and made my body so much younger. And, Leah wasn't under any such influences yet she knew who I was immediately, too, even though I looked to be her junior by at least five years. I mean really, the last time she had seen me I was nearly sixty-years-old. Last week I didn't even look twenty. But, she still knew I was her 'Mom.'

Ever since I had come back home to 1781 from the hospital and the year 2013, I had been getting lightning bursts of memories of my Leah. They were short glimpses, like snapshots flashed in front of my face; of when she was a toddler, holding a dolly in one hand and her blanky in the other; when she was a frustrated teenager, crying about being dumped by a boyfriend; or of the huge grin she sported when she graduated with honors from the nursing program. But, the one clear memory I could hold on to was the feel of her inside of me when I was pregnant, her little feet underneath my right ribcage, pounding away at 3 a.m. every morning. I could have set a clock with her neonatal routine. Hopefully, Rachel had a similar memory she could keep with her forever. And, she really did need to name her.

Rachel stroked the hair down over her daughter's forehead, just like Wallace did with our daughter. "Since she's with Jesus now, I think I'll name her Mary, after His mother. But, I don't want to give her the last name of MacLeod. She's just Mary." Rachel leaned over and kissed her little girl's forehead. "Here, I think I'm ready to let her go. This is just the shell. She's already in heaven. Can I go to sleep now? I'm real tired."

Sarah took the baby from her and said, "You did a great job, Mommy. Get your rest. When you wake up, I'm sure your son will be ready to nurse. That's the one gift Mary was able to give her big brother: a fresh supply of milk."

Now I was the one who was crying. Yeah, right—crying and leaking. "Excuse me, Sarah. Somewhere out there is a baby in need of feeding." I looked down at my wet blouse. "I'll send in Jody with the casket. He and Wallace had it almost finished when I came in."

"Thanks. You did a good job, too. It's hard to think of the right words to say at a time like this, but you did great."

5 The Next Day
August 13, 1781 Pomeroys

It had been an uncomfortably warm night and, even though we had all been splashed or soaked with some form of chaos the day before, we all slept soundly. Grant slept the hardest and longest, which I very much appreciated. Actually, I think we were all grateful for that blessing. He must have been more worn-out than he knew. The two pain pills I had slipped into his sandwich knocked him out for nearly 24 hours. Hey, it worked for me to have that obnoxious and nosy so and so sound asleep and not snooping around the premises, irritating family members with his bad manners. Evidently, no one missed him. I didn't hear of even one person calling for or asking about him!

When Mr. Personality finally awoke the next afternoon, Sarah told him that Rachel couldn't leave for another day, at the earliest. He started to protest but stopped short when he felt a big, heavy hand on his shoulder, not squeezing it, but settling on it firmly. "Let the lass heal," Jody said with authority. "The wee lad will get the attention he needs from the women here until the mother is up and about. Or did ye figure on takin' on that responsibility yerself?" he added with a hint of sarcasm and a double eye blink, his version of a wink.

"Hmph!" Grant grunted then walked away, sweeping his right arm out in a gesture of defiance, using it like a scythe to slice through the laundry bush laden with clouts. He was mad that they couldn't travel right away. And, with two big men living here, he couldn't do anything about it except leave without her.

It didn't seem like he wanted to do that though. I watched him as he sulked away from the house. Rachel was apparently of value to him, an asset of some sort. Why else would he stay and wait for her to recover? I doubt that it was because he cared for her but I suppose that could be a possibility. Yeah, right! That self-centered, oversized, gimme-gimme ingrate cared for no one but himself. She was his trump card for sure but for what game I had no idea. Hopefully, it wasn't one that would bring harm to her or the baby.

Ж

Yesterday I finally got a chance to write my letter to Leah. I had figured out how to send a letter from now, 1781, to an acquaintance in the 21st century. I'm sure James Melbourne, the enchanting young man I met the day I first interacted with Simon, the master time traveler, would forward the letter to my daughter in North Carolina. I'd send a request to my husband's Uncle Tony, also a Melbourne, to hold my letter there in London, not to be read until November 1, 2011.That would be the day after I disappeared, fell off a time portal cliff and broke my back, got dosed with the Fountain of Youth water, and developed a severe case of amnesia. In the letter, I would tell my daughter where I was and not to worry about me, that she now had a new family and that they were some of the 'fictional' characters from the 'Lost' novels.

Rachel was resting comfortably, Baby Boy snuggled amidst a rag quilt in one of my handmade bassinet/ laundry basket containers. Wallace was out in the barn showing Jenny how to weave more of them. We were going to have a bumper crop of corn this year and needed more of the smaller containers for temporary storage until we could get it all processed. I didn't know where Jody was, but Sarah was in the kitchen with me. It was an opportune time to read her my letter and get her opinion about it.

"This first part is for my friend James. I can send it to him through his family on England, for them to pass down through the generations. That way he can break it to Leah gently, what happened to me and where I am:

As of August 4, 2013, Leah is working at the Moses H. Cone Memorial Hospital in Greensboro, not far from our little cafe. She was, will be, my recovery room nurse. So, if you have a chance to talk to her in person, would you please explain this to her and then let her read this letter."

"I hope he gets a chance to meet her in person," I fantasized aloud. "I think they'd get along great. Hmm, I don't think I need to read all of this to you—it's kind of personal in places, but here:

I am alive and well in 1781. I will show up again on August 4, 2013 at the hospital you work in but you will have to let me go back home again to my new family. I have a husband and triplets!"

"So, what do you think?" I asked after reading the selected parts to her. There was no way I was going to let her read the part that a 21st century lady by the name of Lisa Sinclaire had written biographies about her and Jody that were represented as historical romance novels. I didn't want to jinx the possibility that those stories would never be written. I think that I would definitely be interfering with the time line continuum thingy if I did that!

"It sounds like you have all the pertinent information there so James can contact Leah. I'll write a companion letter and send it with my others. I'll ask that someone try and get in touch with her and James, too. That's Moses H. Cone Hospital in Greensboro and August 4, 2013? Wow," she mumbled, "so far away." Sarah regained her composure and added, "That is, if my letters do get through to Barden Hall."

"Now what's this about Barden Hall?" Jody asked brightly as he waltzed into the kitchen. "Oops, sorry," he whispered as he saw the sleeping mother and child a few feet away.

"Aw, she won't wake up until she's ready and neither will he," I commented in my normal speaking voice. I shook my head and added, "It's sure hard to believe that those two are any relation to that Captain Asshole. Did you hear anything about his trial or sentencing?" I asked.

"Weel," Jody said as he pulled out a chair from under the table and sat down, "It looks like he's to be hanged by the neck until daid next, no, wait, that was," Jody counted on his fingers, "he shoulda been hanged yesterday. The major said he didna wanna waste any more food on a man who had tried to take soldiers away from his majesty's army and collected taxes fer his own personal gain. I told him that my son could also give testimony about the um, altercation at the mill, but he said it wasna necessary, that my word and that of his sergeant were enough. And, he wasna too happy about him tryin' to kidnap the lass either," Jody said as he shifted in the seat. "It seems the major has six daughters and is quite protective of them, which is how it should be. So, yer sendin' a letter to Barden Hall so my Benji can watch out fer yer friend James and yer daughter Leah?"

"That's the plan. You know, when the time comes that this letter is to be read, Benji will be quite a bit older than Leah will be. It's been a long time since you've seen him, hasn't it? I'll bet he looks just like you," I proclaimed with parental pride, although I was bragging about someone else's progeny.

"How do ye ken? Did ye ever meet him? Have ye ever been to Barden Hall?" Jody asked excitedly, leaning forward and clutching his knees.

"No, I've never set foot outside the USA, but I do know that he has a tall mama who looks like you and he has red hair, too, so, well, gee, I don't know." I sighed in frustration at getting the man all wound with no way to satisfy his excitement. "I'm sure with his heritage, he's good looking, smart, and responsible."

"Weel, I'll settle for jest bein' responsible. Although with his parents, I'm sure he is the other two as well. Now, do ye think the lass and the bairn can travel tomorrow? They're no bother here and I wouldna want to send her away before she's strong enough."

Sarah looked at Jody, then me, then shrugged her shoulders. "I'll see how's she's doing in the morning and give her my advice. She's been a good patient and the boy's yeast infection seems to be almost gone. It was mostly irritation from being in filthy clouts. I'll make sure she has a change of clothes for him and a few spare clouts with explicit instructions on cleanliness, for her *and* for him. She, um, talked a bit during labor. It seems her mother died before she had a chance to tell her all she needed to know about babies, and, well, a lot of other things. When she gets to feeling better, I'll fill her in on a few other important facts of life. Jody, she said they were headed to stay with family in New Bern. Do you think we can get word to Angus to keep an eye on her?"

Jody grinned as she was asking. "It's already been done; I sent word jest this mornin'. And, I'll make sure Grant kens that I have friends and family from here to New Bern, and that they have all been asked to keep watch over the young lass and the bairn. He may be a nosy man, but I'll bet he kens not to hurt either one of them."

Just then, I heard a crashing noise outside, like stacked wood being knocked over, then the sound of someone running away. "Weel, it looks like he heard what I wanted him to hear," Jody said with a chuckle. "I dinna ken how long he was out there, but he kens now that those two," he nodded to Rachel and Baby Boy, "have protectors from here to the Atlantic Ocean. I'd wager by those squinty eyes that Grant is a family name, not jest a given name. He has the way of the Grants of Leoch about him. Never trust a Grant."

Ж

Wallace saw Grant stumble and fall away from the house. It almost looked, no, he definitely had been listening outside the kitchen window. Jody was in there with the women so there were no worries about them—they were safe. The discourteous traveler now was headed toward him and it looked like he was chanting.

"Leah, Moses Cone, August 4, 2013, Leah, Moses Cone, oh yeah, Greensboro, August...crap, I have to find a way to write this down. I'll never remember so many things that don't make sense," Grant mumbled. He looked up and saw the tall, young father staring at him. "Hmph," he snorted and turned to head in the opposite direction. "Leah, Moses, Greensboro, August 4, 2013. Leah, Moses..."

Ж

Later that day

We got an unexpected guest this afternoon. Young Hannah Althouse came by for a visit. She had been with the Donaldson family since March and was on her way home to her 'first' family.

"I don't know if I can be away from my babies for very long," she admitted to Sarah. "I wanted to learn the healin' from you, but do you think that maybe we can wait until winter? I mean, there's so much to do with the garden, and the girls are a handful for just Mrs. Donaldson, and I already miss my boys, and," she sighed deeply, "I haven't even been gone one day. Did you know that they crawl now? Well, not really crawl, but they can roll over and over to get whatever they want. We had to put the chairs down sideways in front of the hearth. The fire has been out, but they like the coolness—there's a draft that comes down the chimney. We don't want them going in there later when there's a fire going!"

Young Hannah was all aglow talking about her 'boys.' The twins weren't related to her, but she had been their au pair since they were born. "Oh, and look at this," she said as she held out a little purse. "Miranda made it for me for my birthday. She didn't know what date it was so said I could have it now. It was late if my day had passed, but otherwise it would be an early birthday present. Wasn't that sweet? And get this," she said with unbridled enthusiasm, "it *was* my birthday! And I hadn't told anyone!" Tears were starting to build up on her bottom eyelids. "I think I'd better go home and see my Ma and Pa for a few days. But, I'm going to ask them if it's okay if I go back again. The Donaldson's need me and," she sniffed and wiped her nose and eyes with the back of her hand, "I need them. We're all born into a family, but sometimes God gives you a different one later. Do you know what I mean?"

"Boy, howdy," I replied with emphasis. "I mean, yes, I do know because it happened to me, too. I do believe we're both doubly blessed."

"And there's no hurry on the schooling. We're going to be busy here building another house for Wallace and Evie and their children so I wouldn't have too much time for you until this winter anyhow."

"See, God's got it all under control," I bragged. "Hey, I'll bet you'd like to see the babies. They're right over there. I have to go see what Wallace and Jenny are up to. They've been quiet too long."

Just then, a crash came from the barn. "I'm okay," hollered Jody from inside of it.

"Well, I'll go see what happened anyway," Sarah said with exasperation. "That man has nine lives to be sure, but I don't want him using up one of them with an infection. I'm going to go look for broken skin."

Sarah and I left for the barn, chuckling like the two sisters we had become, laughing at the skill and adroitness of Jody the swordsman who could still be clumsy just turning around in tight quarters, his broad shoulders knocking pictures off a wall or pitchers off a table.

Ж

Grant had been watching the get-together of the Pomeroy women and the young girl. The lass was alone now. Maybe she knew how to write. He walked over to her, wearing the smile that he saved for important occasions. "Good day, miss," he said pleasantly. "Are you here for long?"

"No," Hannah said cautiously. There was something amiss about a man who came up to a stranger, especially a young woman, and started talking to her without a proper introduction.

"Can you write?" he demanded.

"Yes, sir," she said softly. She looked around but didn't see anyone. This man scared her and being alone with him was even more frightening. Her whole body was frozen: she was too terrified to yell. What if he killed her before anyone could find her?

"Good! Then you're comin' with me," he said, grabbing her arm as she pulled away from him. He had a tight grip, though, and dragged her by her elbow up the steps into the kitchen. "Sit there," he growled hoarsely, trying not to be too loud. Rachel and the baby were still asleep and he didn't want to wake them. Rachel would be no problem—he could handle her, but that nosy, curly haired healer and that other woman would come in to check on them if they knew that she or the baby were awake.

Earlier, he had noticed the fancy quill pen and paper in the cupboard. This family didn't have much and he wasn't going to steal these—he was just borrowing them. He opened the cabinet, took them out, and then thrust them at the girl. "You write what I tell you. And if you don't," he said menacingly, "I'll get you." He drew his finger across his throat like it was a knife. "And don't tell anyone about this, you hear?"

"Yes, sir," she squeaked softly. Her throat was so tight from fear that she probably wouldn't have been able to yell even if she had seen someone nearby.

"Get Leah at the Moses Hospital in Greensboro, that's North Carolina, on August 4th two thousand thirteen. Okay? Now read it back."

Hannah took a minute to finish writing what he had said. "Get Leah at the Moses Hospital in Greensboro that's North

Carolina on August for two thousand thirteen," Hannah said in a whisper, then cautiously looked up at him to see if she had the words right.

The mean-looking man shifted his eyes back and forth, as if he was thinking about something, and then rubbed his chin. "Now write this down, too. 'Go get Benji at Barden Hall, Scotland in 1990. He has the treasure.' Now read it back!" he growled this time, as if he was mad.

Hannah finished the words then read them back to him. "Go get Benny at Barden Hall Scotland end nineteen ninety. He has the treasure."

"That's Benji, you idiot, not Benny!" he yelled.

Rachel started moving with the sudden loud noise and the baby began to cry. "Give me that," he snorted as he grabbed the still wet paper. He stuffed the cork into the inkwell and grabbed the quill, stuffing both of them haphazardly back into the cabinet. "Now, get out of here and don't you tell anyone that you did the writing for me, you hear?" He glared at her and moved his finger across his neck with that ominous throat-slashing gesture, then rushed out the door, around to the patch of scrub wood at the back of the house.

Grant kept the house in sight as he sat down to look at the parchment. This was going to be so sweet: revenge on the Pomeroys for killing his brother. They may not have been the ones who actually put the noose around Atholl's neck, but he wouldn't have been caught if it hadn't been for them. And, there was still that major soldier man who believed everything that Jody and his son Wallace told him—he'd get him, too. Grant turned the paper over in his hands to make sure he didn't smudge it any more than it already was. He'd have to figure a way to get this letter to his son, if he ever had one. He'd heard about fairies, how they could travel to the past and to the future. The Big Red One's grandson must be a fairy if he was alive in 1990. And, the other woman, Evie, the young tall man's wife: she had said that her daughter was her nurse in the hospital in 2013. How could a daughter nurse the mother? Grant shook his head. These fairies were queer ones. But, he didn't care if he had to wait over 200 years for revenge. He was going to make sure that this Benji was killed for what his grandfather and uncle did to his brother.

And, now he knew what the grandson looked like, sort of. A tall, red-haired man in that small town of Barden Hall shouldn't be too hard to find. But first, this Benji would have to suffer like Atholl did. Surely, there was someone in the year 1990 who would like to carve little bits of body parts off the man. If he thought that he could get close enough to this Big Red One, he'd do it to him, too. He shook his head again. Nah, he'd let his son's sons do it. He looked down at his crotch and frowned. Okay, he'd let his brother's son's sons do it. He'd take little Atholl, Jr. as his own, just to make sure that his revenge was satisfied. Yes, if he started early, he could make sure the boy got the message. He patted the folded paper. He would make sure that it was passed on to his children's children's children until Benji was done in and the 'treasure' was found. Who knows? Maybe by that time Benji and his family really would have all the gold and gems that he'd let his heirs believe they had.

Ж

Rachel woke up to a new person in the room. "Hi," she said sweetly to the girl who looked to be her own age.

"Hi," Hannah squeaked then sniffed repeatedly, trying to keep the tears of fear from falling.

"Are you okay?" Rachel asked.

Hannah didn't say anything, but stood there, mute, and terrified. Rachel recognized the signs of intimidation. There was only one person on this property who would do that to a young woman. "Was there a man in here that scared you?" she asked although she already knew it had to be what had happened.

Hannah nodded her head and her tears stopped. It looked like she had a friend who understood what she couldn't say.

"Did he hit you?" Rachel asked as she sat up.

Baby Atholl Junior was making little mewing noises as he awoke. Instinctively, Hannah went to him, picked him up, and rubbed his back. She looked at the girl in the bed and asked, "Is he yours?"

Rachel nodded and dropped her arm out of the sleeve of the hospital gown and reached for her son. She bared her breast and started suckling him. "He scared you though, didn't he?" she asked.

Hannah nodded then put her index finger up to her throat and imitated the neck slashing motion that Grant had threatened her with.

Rachel closed her eyes with the painful bliss that was her son nursing for the first time in nearly a day. Her milk was starting to come in; she could feel it. She reached her hand out to the frightened girl next to her. "I won't let him hurt you," she said strongly as she clasped her hand, "I'll kill him first."

Hannah was shocked at the words, but even more so at the fire in the very young mother's eyes. She looked to be her own age but had the iron jaw set of a warrior. She believed that this woman really would kill that mean man if he tried to hurt her. "Uh, okay, thank you," she said and nodded. "I don't really like sayin' it, but that makes me feel better."

Rachel's glare of hatred for her brother melted to compassion for the new friend she had just made by threatening to kill her own kin. Well, he was worth getting rid of. But first, she had to figure out how to do it.

6 Marty's Dilemma

August 18, 1781
Lost in North Carolina

*M*arty Melbourne was on his own now. He had left the four others back at the impromptu camp he had helped set up. Ian Kincaid had been seriously wounded: a hatchet gash to the neck and a botched castration. His young son, Wee Ian, had been beaten, but was alive, willing, and capable of taking care of his wounded father's needs. Marty's son, James, and his wife, Leah, were there also. The newlywed couple had traveled 'back' in time from 2013 to help him here in 1781. Soon they would be on their way to live with her mother, Evie. Evie was another time traveler and married to Ian's cousin Wallace, the son of Jody Pomeroy, Scottish-born soldier, farmer, and American patriot. Evie had undergone a mysterious age reversal so now appeared younger than her adult daughter, Leah.

Only last week Marty had sent the cryptic letter requesting James's assistance in this time era, hoping that the sealed epistle would make it to London. He had given instructions with the letter that it be held in trust at the House of Lords until 2013. At that time, it was to be delivered to James's post office box. Evidently, all had gone according to plan. James and Leah had arrived yesterday and had given Ian Kincaid the blood transfusion needed to save his life. The act gave substance to the Cherokee Indian legend of the Nûñnë'hĩ, the 'fairy,' who had come and put his spirit into Star Walker, Ian Kincaid, in order to heal his broken body. Now, Ian would live to sire the child, Scout Kincaid, who would become his son James's ancestor.

So, now that his son's heritage had been assured, he could go back to the 21st century to be with the lad's mother, Bibb, the woman he should have married decades ago. He could also meet the son he never knew he had, Billy Burke. Bibb had secretly birthed then given up for adoption their love child, her first-born son. Bibb now had liver cancer and needed to undergo a liver transplant. Yes, Marty desperately wanted to go back 'home' to the 21st century. But first, he had to find his way back to the time portal, The Trees that marked the magnetic anomaly that facilitated time travel. He already had the other two factors needed to complete the journey: the rare Greek coin and a focus person in the targeted time period, his beloved Bibb.

"Well, I *thought* this was the right direction," Marty said to his horse. "At least I remember the creek was on my right and the morning sun was in my eyes on my way in. Crap! You're turned around, Melbourne! You're supposed to be going the opposite direction of how you got here! Stop daydreaming about your homecoming and find those trees!"

Marty got off the horse and led her to the creek, allowing her to drink and graze while he pulled out the map and rechecked his location. After ten minutes of looking at the map, turning it 90 degrees, looking at the course of the creek, turning the map again and looking at the creek still again, he decided to take a short nap. "Stay," he said to the horse and grabbed a short length of soft rope out of his saddlebag to hobble her. "We still have a ways to go, but I can't think straight. I didn't sleep a wink last night and it's creeping up on me. Hopefully, a nap will clear my head because if I don't get us lined out and started in the right direction, we'll wind up at the Pomeroy's before Leah and James. And, I'm not even heading that way! Hmph!"

Marty took the bedroll off the back of the mare and used it as a pillow, setting his tricorner hat on his head sideways to block the splotchy sunrays coming through the tree branches. His frowning face transitioned into a contented grin. Tomorrow night, he'd be lying down with Bibb at his side, or even closer…

Ж

"What the…!" Marty shouted, his hand inadvertently knocking his hat away from his eyes. He had been asleep, that much he knew, but someone was trying to pull his bedroll out from under his head.

"Stay still if you know what's good for ya!" the gapped tooth man instructed. He jerked the bedroll out from under Marty's head with one hand and twirled the carved bone handle of his knife menacingly with the other. "I just want to see what you have for me here," he added with a snort, finishing his report with a wad of spittle a scant foot from Marty's face.

Marty gingerly scooted up to a seated position, keeping one eye on the highwayman, and looked to see if anyone else was with him. Bandits usually traveled in groups of three or more. He couldn't see or hear anyone other than a teenaged girl with a baby, squatted down by the creek. She wasn't paying attention to what was going on with the robber, his knife, or him. She was dipping her bare bottomed son in the water, laughing at his giggles as he kicked his feet into the slow moving, warm current.

Marty looked back up at the thief and felt braver. It was only one man and a knife—he could handle this scenario. "Did you find what you were looking for?" he asked sarcastically. He knew there wasn't anything but a blanket in his bedroll. He didn't think it wise to have a lot of money with him so hadn't traveled with more than a few shillings and those sewn into his vest lining.

The man answered with a sneer, "As a matter of fact I did." He re-rolled the blanket, hastily tied it together, and stood up. "Take off your boots," he commanded.

Marty's eyes cut to the woman and the baby at the water's edge. They weren't involved in the theft, but they were probably traveling with him. The young pair wouldn't be on the road alone; there weren't any homes nearby, and he hadn't seen a wagon or any horses. "Shit," Marty mumbled as he pulled off his right boot, hoping that he hadn't cut his hand enough to bleed. He was trying to palm his hidden boot knife and had sliced himself in the process.

"What d'ya mean 'shit'?" the man asked.

"Shit: you're taking my boots and I'll bet you're seriously considering taking my horse, too," Marty said to cover his fumbled cursing.

"Oh, so you're a betting man, are ya?" Grant asked snidely. "Well, I'll bet this morning you didn't see your day finding you barefoot and without a horse by noon, did ya?" The raggedy man picked up the boots and dropped one of them beside his foot, estimating the fit potential. They looked to be bigger than the ones that he had on but that didn't seem to bother him. He picked the boot back up and stuffed it under his arm. "Rachel, bring the horse over here," he called.

Marty watched as the girl threw the laughing baby over her shoulder, his bare butt exposed to the sunshine, his little feet pedaling with glee. She walked twenty yards to grab the reins of the horse that was only ten feet from the robber. She bent down and loosened the knot on the hobble rope with one hand as she clutched her child to her with the other. She didn't say a word as she handed him the reins, but did cut her eyes to Marty. It didn't look like she was any happier with this scenario than he was.

"See what he has in his saddlebags," Grant commanded gruffly. He walked a few steps away from Marty and grinned as he moved his knife through the air flamboyantly, almost asking his victim to attack him—he wanted a fight.

Marty subconsciously gulped then looked to the girl. She was dispassionately pulling the straps off his flat saddlebag. There was nothing in it; he had given all of his food and cookware to Wee Ian. He only had his canteen and a pocketful of granola. She flipped up the flap on the bag and stood on tiptoes to look inside, confirming what she already knew—it was empty. "Looks like he has even less than we do," she commented idly then walked away from the humble nag, back towards the creek.

"Where is it?" Grant demanded. "No one travels without food or a way to get it. You don't even have a pan to cook with? Nah, somethin' fishy's goin' on here."

"You're right," Marty said with a twinkle in his eye. Even in dire straits, he couldn't pass up the opportunity to make a joke. He took off his hat and pulled out the small fishing lure with the twisted line attached to it. "Fishy. I eat fish: fish for breakfast, fish for lunch, and fish for dessert after I've had my fish for supper!

Smack! Grant didn't think much of Marty's wit and used the back of his hand to tell him so.

Marty was knocked for a loop, literally, landing face down in the dirt with the backhanded slap. He rolled over cautiously; making sure his knife was still hidden and hadn't been revealed in the unexpected assault. Marty rubbed his jaw and asked, "Now what'd you go and do that for? I'll share the fish. I mean, if you and your wife are hungry, I'll see what I can scare up. Although, it might be more lucrative if we waited until sundown."

"She's not my wife—she's my stupid sister," Grant snorted. "And what in the hell is Luke ruh tive?"

"Oh, it's just a Scottish word that means you catch more fish when the sun isn't high," Marty answered, making sure he didn't smile at his lame fabrication. The man was obviously unschooled on top of being short tempered. Hopefully, he'd just take the boots and horse and leave—leave him with his life. Marty suddenly panicked at the thought of dying.

"Well, I don't speak Scottish and I don't like to eat fish. But, I will take this hat and the hook and line. She can catch fish for herself. I'll eat this," he said as he pulled out a fat tortilla wrapped sandwich from his pocket and waved it around, showing off his bounty.

"You said all the food was gone, Grant," hollered Rachel as she made her way back up from the creek, stomping her bare feet angrily.

"I lied," Grant sneered then took a big bite of the ham and cheese fare. He tossed the hat he had taken from Marty down to her. "Here, there's a hook and line on it; go catch yourself a fish. Oh, and you can keep the hat. I still like this one best," he said as he tapped the dusty crown of his black silk edged tricorner hat. "It always looked better on me than Atholl anyhow."

Rachel huffed in disgust but took the hat and carefully pulled out the hook. "Come on, Junior, we'll have better luck with a hook, I promise." She looked over at Marty, trying to decide if she should give him back his hat or not, then glanced up at the high noon sky. She would probably look odd wearing a man's hat but Grant had taken hers and she didn't want it back after what he had done to it. "Hey, it's softer than the leaves and I had the runs from the food that those Pomeroys fed me. You can wash it out in the creek—it'll be as good as ever.

Rachel settled the hat that was one size too big on her head and caught Marty's eye. She didn't dare speak to him but lowered her eyes, saying, 'I'm sorry but I need it,' with her expression. Marty bit back the words, 'It looks cute on you.' She wouldn't have understood his odd sense of humor and her brother would probably use the uninvited conversation with his sister as an excuse to hit him again. Instead, Marty bent his head and prayed silently that he would get out of this predicament with his life. He just wanted to go home. He glanced up to heaven and added silently, 'And in one piece would be nice, too, Lord.'

"Hurry up and catch your fish. We should be able to make New Bern in two days if you don't…"

"Oh, keep your pants on," Rachel answered sassily, cutting off his admonishment. She wrapped up the hook and line and stuck it back on the hat brim. "They won't be biting until later, anyhow. Let me have a couple of bites of that sandwich and then we can leave."

"Gettin' a bit chatty in your old age there, aren't you?" Grant barked back, twirling his knife haft between thumb and index finger menacingly. "Here, I saved you a bite," he said, and threw the last bit of sandwich at her, intentionally tossing it short so it landed in the dirt.

Rachel glared at him but picked up the soiled bit of tortilla with a couple of bits of cheese and mayonnaise still stuck to it. She carefully pulled the dirt and grassy pieces away from it and nibbled at the morsel, savoring the bite. She stuck the tip of her tongue through her lips, removing a pebble that she had missed. She plopped the rest of the sandwich into her mouth, suddenly afraid that Grant would take the meager meal away from her. "Let's go," she said with her cheeks full. "He won't follow us," she added then looked over at Marty, telling him with her eyes to stay put if he knew what was good for him.

Grant looked over at his victim and crowed, "Well, I don't think he'll be going too far without these boots." He turned his heel and showed off the purloined footwear to Marty, "or these, either." Grant took his worn out boots and stuffed them into the saddlebag. "And I think I ought to ride the horse for a bit. You know how new shoes always give me blisters," then swung up on the horse. He trotted the horse a few yards down the deer path then called back snidely to the stern faced woman-child trying to catch up with him, "And don't dawdle—we have a long ways to go until sundown."

Marty sighed in relief at his close call. He didn't care about the horse; he was going to let her go anyway. However, the ground was rocky and his feet were as soft as a baby's. "Shoot, I'd be better off if I could walk on my hands. At least they're calloused!" He turned over his hands and looked at his palms in frustration. "New Bern?" he asked himself, suddenly changing his focus from the dilemma of his newly attained tenderfoot status.

"They won't be there in a few days; that's probably 200 miles away. It looks like someone is even more lost than I am."

Marty lifted the rock at the base of the tree where he had stashed the map just before taking his nap. "Gee, and I just wanted to make sure it didn't blow away," he said to himself, grateful once again at his good fortune. "Okay, okay, I get it, Lord, You've got my attention. Thanks for saving my bacon, I mean, thanks for saving my life today. And please, please, please, please, get me back to my time and Bibb safely. And, guide those doctors doing the transplant and make sure they put the right parts in the right person and, well, You know what I need and please, just help me to listen to what You want me to do; in Jesus name, Amen. Oh, and would you look out for that girl, Rachel, and her baby, too? Thanks, Amen again."

Marty spread the map out on the ground. "Okay, Lord, I'm looking at it with You right here next to me." He grinned as he realized that there really was Divine intervention in his map reading. He had forgotten that he had coded his map by turning the coordinates 180 degrees so that north was south and east was west. "Gotcha! Thanks."

Marty stood to start his trek to the trees and was quickly reminded of his other dilemma: no boots. "Crap!" he cursed mildly then looked around. "Well, at least you have the knife," he told himself. He looked around at his surroundings, trying to find something, anything, that he could use as shoes. He looked down at his pants. Yes, he could fabricate something from strips of the brown denim duck that he had chosen over the homespun wool the re-enactors had suggested. "These are close enough in looks and will wear for years if I need them to," he told the seamstress. He never thought that he'd have to cut them down for sandals though.

"Sandals! That's it." Marty picked his steps carefully as he walked to the still, shallow area of the creekside. He pushed aside some reeds and yanked a tuft out of the mud. He tried to pull the long leaf apart lengthwise but couldn't. Yes, they would be suitable. He'd never woven a basket but these grasses seemed tough enough to braid and stitch into soles. He bent to the task, selecting the midsize reeds as his weaving material. He cut a few of the young shoots, too, and brought the green bundle to his little dayroom under the tree. "Lunch!" he exclaimed as he stuck the soft, tender end of a young reed into his mouth, biting the succulent portion and chewing his micro salad carefully before he bent to his work. Just because he'd never made shoes, didn't mean he couldn't accomplish the task. He'd just never been motivated. And, getting back to his family, Bibb and the son he never even knew he had, was plenty of motivation.

Marty braided a pair of two-yard-long reed switches, making sure he kept them the same width and density. He wound each whip into a long oval then set a rock on top of each to flatten and secure them. He hastily carved a needle out of a hardwood branch and used it with a length of tough grass as cording to stitch the concentric rows of braided reeds together. "Thank You, thank You, thank You," he praised over and over again as he worked at his cobbler task. He glanced up at the sun and saw that it was almost evening. Should he leave now or wait until tomorrow? "Duh!" he said aloud. "Remember what taking a break did for you today!" he shuddered, recalling Grant. Something was definitely wrong with the man. Too bad his little sister and nephew had to tag along with him.

7 The Right Road Home

August 19, 1781
Somewhere in North Carolina

"Okay, I know this is the right road, I know this is the right road, I know this is the right road," Marty chanted as he trudged down the familiar path—or so he thought. All the bushes, trees, and hills were beginning to look alike.

"This has to be the right road, this has to be the right road, please, Lord, let this be the right road," he prayed, his lips cracked from thirst. He didn't want to take a drink yet; he was conserving the water in his canteen. He had tanked up before leaving the creek, knew that his constant chattering was drying his mouth, but his soul and sanity needed his mantra more than his mouth and body needed water.

"So close, so close," he babbled softly, suddenly unsure if he *was* on the right road. The daylight was gone, but he knew the moon had been full three days ago and would be rising soon. Marty stopped where he was and debated with himself, wordlessly in order to save his saliva, about the wisdom of proceeding rather than resting. The afterglow of the sunset was gone. He knew how easy it would be to get turned around without his solar guide. It would be wise of him to sit and wait for moonrise: wise, but not what he wanted to do. He pivoted in a tight circle to check the area one more time and suddenly became confused, disoriented, and afraid. "Okay, okay; I hear you, Lord. I'll sit and wait for your lunar compass to come up."

Marty plopped down right where he stood, too scared to venture even the scant ten yards to his left to sit beneath the trees.

He would be more comfortable leaning up against one of the sturdy sentinels but he was afraid to venture from where he was. He didn't want to chance heading the wrong direction, or walk in circles, or go back to where he had been robbed. He shuddered. Or bump into Grant and that bone-handled knife of his that he seemed so eager to employ.

Marty decided it was best to remain where he was—seated in between two stands of locust bushes, scrubby oversized weeds that looked just like the hundreds of others he had passed. Everything looked the same; it was no wonder he was lost.

He shifted his weight, but it didn't do any good. His bony butt was painfully parked on the sharp, rocky gravel that was everywhere—there was no way to get comfortable. He accepted his lot, sighed in temporary defeat, then carefully slipped off his sandals. He set them on the ground in front of him, pointing them, he hoped, in the direction he was to take when he resumed his journey. But, before he went any further, he *had* to take a short nap. He set his forehead down on his knobby knees and breathed deeply, trying to avert the panic that was sneaking in. "I'll be okay, I'll be okay," he chanted until he finally fell asleep, his hands falling lax to his sides, his body gently tumbling sideways to slumber soundly in the fetal position.

Marty slept hard and dreamed of kisses on his cheek. His beloved Bibb was giving him quick little chicken pecks, gradually increasing her ardor until she was licking the entire side of his face, leaving his smiling cheek wet with slobber...

Marty sucked in a lungful of wet, dusty air, awaking from his surreal dream, and realized where he was: lost.

The sky was rumbling, the growling thunder echoing against the low clouds that had rolled in while he slept. The firmament was a constantly changing pallet of blacks, grays, and whites. The lightning bolts streaked horizontally across the sky, rarely striking the earth, instead stretching and clawing their way across the pulsing panorama. The heavy rain was now coming in at him sideways, first one direction then suddenly changing courses. Marty looked over at the trees and briefly reconsidered seeking shelter under them. "Hmph," he snorted and shook his head, "that's all I need: to get struck by lightning."

So Marty, now rested and recharged, stayed where he was and made the best of his situation. He put a few more rocks on top of his sandals to make sure they weren't turned askew or blown away completely. He'd need his woven reed direction indicators pointing in the right direction when daylight finally came. He grabbed a few more stones and propped up his canteen, hoping to catch some of the sporadic, teaspoon-sized raindrops that were coming in at odd angles, not 'dropping' straight down.

Marty stood up, took off all of his clothes, and employed his shirt as a washrag to scrub the stink of the past two-week's journey off his body. He danced in the rain, glad that he could both stand and move. "Thanks for the shower, Lord," he sang as he twirled. He gathered as much moisture as he could into the shirt and pants and rubbed them together in a vain attempt at cleaning them.

Marty danced, and washed, and sang until he was worn out with his praises. "Ah, a good attitude will get you through tough times and woe more than any amount of money," he gloated. "And I'll be a bit less gamey when I *do* get back into town!" he declared positively.

Marty grinned as he remembered that he still had some granola stashed in the pocket of his leather vest. "Thanks for the food, too," he crowed as he grabbed a couple of morsels and popped them into his mouth.

The brief downpour was a warm summer cloudburst that hadn't chilled the air. "Thanks again," a worn out and satisfied Marty said softly as he snuggled his face and chest into his wadded up clothing, finding comfort in the warm, moist and musky cotton.

This time, it was a foot poking him in his backside that woke him. Marty was too at peace with himself to be frightened by the intrusion so, rather than panic, he stretched out his arms, grinned at the glow of sunrise visible in front of him, and slowly stood up. He totally ignored the fact that there had to be a person or animal attached to the fanny prod that had roused him. He looked away from the sunrise and turned around to see his wake up crew: three Indians and four ponies, one of them his stolen mare, complete with saddle.

"Looks like you found my horse," he said, smiling and nodding to each of the men in greeting. "If you care to help me find my way home, I'll be glad to let you keep her…"

Marty could tell that his words weren't understood. He could just as easily been reciting the months of the year to these braves: they didn't seem interested. What they were interested in, at least the tallest of the group, were his clothes.

Red Shirt tilted his head in confusion then kicked the bundle of clothing away from Marty's feet. He picked up the shirt first, shook it out and examined it, sniffed it, made a face of disgust, then threw it back down. He squatted beside the pants, ran his fingers over the brass buttons on the fly, and smiled. He stood up with the tan, heavyweight cotton, work pants, held them in front of his hips to check the fit, and then frowned. He poked the brass studs with his index finger, taken aback by the rivets at the pockets. He wanted to make sure they weren't bugs, or so it seemed.

"Those are to reinforce the seams," Marty volunteered, then employed sign language, pulling imaginary cloth to show how sturdy the stitching was.

Marty turned slightly to see what the other two braves were doing. "My shoes!" he screeched in panic. He had been distracted with Red Shirt and the jeans and now saw that the other two braves each held one of his handmade sandals, turning them over, examining the crude workmanship, chuckling at his

58

primitive efforts. "Where were they?" he asked in dread. "I have to know which direction...oh, bother," he finished in exasperation, "what difference does it make now? I don't even know if I was going in the right direction to start with."

Red Shirt was now smiling. He had figured out that the pants weren't insect infested and would make sturdy wear for him. He bent over sideways and untied the knot on the thong holding up his loincloth. He ceremoniously pulled the thin strip of leather belting away, bowed apart his knees, letting his breechclout drop to the ground. He took two steps away and sat on the ground, trying to put the pants on over his moccasins.

Marty pulled himself in emotionally and evaluated his current situation in a clinical, detached manner, seeing it as it really was. This could play out to his benefit or wind up with his death. The horse and clothes, or lack thereof, would only be a short-term inconvenience for him if the Indians 'appropriated' them. He could 'give' them to them and be on his way with maybe some good directions to The Trees. Or, he could make a big stink over a bit of cloth and horseflesh and wind up dead, laid out in itty bitty pieces as a fall feast for the crows. 'No contest,' he thought.

"Here, let me show you a trick," Marty suggested as he walked over, still bare butt naked, to become the personal dresser to the Indian brave in charge.

Evidently, Marty's good nature showed through because Red Shirt stopped his struggle and let his paleface valet take over. "Here, take off the moccasins first," he instructed, pointing to Red Shirt's moccasins, but not touching them lest he find out the hard way that it was an insult. Red Shirt kicked them off then looked up for instructions on what to do next. "Here, stand up," Marty said, offering his hand to the charismatic red man.

Red Shirt didn't accept the hand but stood up unaided—cutting his eyes over to his men to make sure he hadn't lost their respect in dealing with the white man. If they had, they sure weren't showing it; both of them were stone-faced and intrigued with the metal studded trousers. "See, you get one foot in, pull it up a little then put the other foot in…there you go. Now just shimmy them up," Marty pantomimed, causing all three of the braves to chuckle softly at his getting dressed without any clothes.

"Now the buttons—be careful. You don't want to get your bits and pieces caught in there." Marty illustrated by holding his private parts behind one hand, pretending to fumble with imaginary buttons with the other. Now the men were laughing out loud as Red Shirt stuffed his hand down his pants, making sure he was all inside before pulling the stiff fabric buttonholes around the brass buttons. It took a full minute for him to get them all fastened but everyone cheered when he raised his head with a guttural shout of victory at his accomplishment.

"You look mighty fine there," Marty complemented then bowed his head briefly to accentuate the remark. "Um, do you think that I might keep the shirt?" he asked, tentatively picking it up, sniffing it like Red Shirt had, and making his own exaggerated look of disgust at the smell—it really was quite rank.

Red Shirt laughed at his antics and moved his hand as if he was shooing a bug off a biscuit: yes, Marty could keep the shirt; he didn't want it. Marty said, "Thanks," and donned the shirt quickly before anyone else could lay claim to it.

Red Shirt said something in his native language. Marty wasn't an expert on American Indians but this was Bibb's ancestor's land. He was probably speaking Cherokee. But, knowing, or making an educated guess, at which tongue he was speaking, didn't make understanding him any easier. Marty shrugged his shoulders in the universally understood, he hoped, gesture of 'I don't know what you mean.'

Red Shirt grinned; he knew the man didn't understand him, but he was fun to watch. Most white men were all the same; this one was different. He'd let him keep his old breechclout and the shirt. He didn't want to shame him but did want his pants. Red

60

Shirt pointed to the cloth on the ground, offering it to the silly man.

"For me? Really? Now that's mighty considerate." Marty picked up the decorated breechclout, very clean he was relieved to see, and nodded, "Thanks!" He bent over and grabbed the leather thong then looked at the men. "Let's see if I can figure this out...," he said as he held up the thong with one hand and the cloth with the other. He smiled and shrugged in resignation at what was sure to be a one-man comedy show.

Marty bent over to the humiliating task. First, he lifted his shirt, unavoidably flashing the men with his nakedness, and tied the thong around his waist. He hoped he wasn't making too much a fool of himself trying to figure out how to weave the cloth up between his legs and in and over the leather waistband in the front then, Lord help him, up his backside. "Well, let's see if this feeble old white man can figure out how to cover his ass like an Indian," Marty joked, making broad gestures as he made a show of his lack of skill in dressing Cherokee-style. It was better to make a parody and entertain the men than stress about his lack of clothing and loss of dignity.

Marty fought the fabric and leather then realized that his main problem was the shirt—it kept getting in the way. "I still want this so don't anyone take it, uh, please," he said sincerely. He pulled his shirt off over his head. The thong still tied around his waist but the butt flap was only tucked in under his navel. Marty knew the braves were still laughing at him and now that he had the shirt off, he realized how simple the task should have been. "There!" he crowed in victory as he danced a little two step in a tight circle to show them that he had managed to cover himself adequately, at least as far as he was concerned. "Thank you, thank you very much," he added with an Elvis Presley impersonation, "I'll be here all day."

His voice changed back to his regular light British accent as he asked, "Are you from around here? I mean, I'm lost and need some help getting to the big trees." Marty was employing his own version of sign language but it didn't seem to help. "I want to get back to my woman and son," he said with sadness. He put his arms in front of him and drew a curvy figure in the air, then placed his hands on the front of his chest to indicate big breasts and mimed cradling a baby. He realized that tears were falling down his cheeks but he didn't care. He wanted to be back with Bibb and to meet the son he never knew he had. And right now, it didn't look like his chances to be with them were very good. Nope, they were slim to none.

Nope, not none. Marty looked up to the sky and put his arms up in prayer. "Lord, would you help these strong men understand that I need to go home? I don't mean them any harm but really could use a bit of food, water, and direction. I'd appreciate it; in Jesus name, Amen."

Red Shirt snorted an order and the younger of the braves retrieved a bag from his horse. The three men sat down in an open circle and motioned for Marty to sit with them. The young man handed each one a modest-sized chunk of jerky, then passed around the canteen of water. It appeared that two out of three of his prayer requests had been answered. "Just a minute," Marty said as he rifled through his vest to retrieve his contribution to the meal. "Here." Marty offered each of the men a cashew nut then took one for himself. "Mmm, good."

Each of the men sniffed the nut. Red Shirt, being the bravest of the braves, ventured a lick of it. "Hmph." Evidently, the salty taste appealed to him because he popped the whole nut in his mouth and chewed away blissfully, grunting to his peers to try theirs.

"I wish I had more to share but I didn't plan on being gone this long. Then again, I didn't plan on being without my horse either. You do know that," he nodded with his forehead to his mare, "*that* is my horse."

Red Shirt didn't say anything. He knew what the white man was saying. He didn't doubt that the horse had been his recently. The man he took it from didn't fit in the saddle—the stirrups were too low for him. He was also mean to her, kicking the mare and racing her in circles just to stir up dust around the woman and child. No, the horse probably belonged to Dances Naked, but now she was his.

"You can keep the horse," Marty offered, although he knew they didn't understand him. "I'm very grateful for the food and drink, and the new clothes are nice, too," he said as he fingered the front of the breechclout. "But what I'd really appreciate is direction. Now, you see, there are these trees—they're very special. You go through them here," he said as he poked a couple of limb bits into little piles of gravel. He 'walked' with the first two fingers of his right hand through the tree models, "and then, *poof*, you come out…" Marty pulled his hand away and brought it out around the other side of him, fluttering his fingers like they were wayward moths.

Red Shirt's eyes widened. He knew where these trees were. Yes, he'd send Dances Naked in the right direction. He said he wanted to be with his woman and child. If he was willing to go through The Trees to be with them, he'd help him. But he wasn't going with him. That was where he lost his brother many winters ago. Little Big Man went into them to show how brave he was, but he never came out.

Marty saw the momentary look of terror on Red Shirt's face. He wasn't sure if the man understood his English or if it was just his sign language, but he knew one thing for sure: Red Shirt knew where he wanted to go.

Just as Marty was deciding how he should broach the subject—he didn't know anything about Cherokee diplomacy—the horses started neighing and jumping around. Something was frightening them.

"You can have the mare, but I want that stallion," Grant announced menacingly as he strutted into the middle of the group, brandishing the bone-handled knife in his left hand, a silvery pistol in his right.

All of the men in the breakfast club looked at each other, completely bypassing looks of embarrassment or anger at being caught off guard, instead making non-spoken plans to disarm the dishonorable white man. Red Shirt looked at Marty, too. Marty lowered his eyelids halfway, letting his new friend know that he was on their side. He'd help them take down the man who had stolen his horse, hat, and boots, and hit him in the face for no reason at all.

"Where'd you get the gun, Grant?" Marty called out sassily, meaning to distract the repeat offending villain from whatever the braves were doing.

"My dumb sister had it, if it's any of your business, and it's not," he replied indignantly. "Now, why don't you be a good little man and bring me the reins of that stallion there," he ordered Marty.

Marty stood up slowly, taking as much time as he dared. He wasn't part of the action; he was the diversion. He pulled himself up to his full height and brushed a few leaves off the front of his breechclout. He was an older man but still much taller than Grant. "Little?" Marty asked as he stuck his neck out proudly. *'Hurry up, red men. Lord, don't let him shoot that gun, but if he does, may he be a lousy shot!'*

"What's going on here?" Grant asked gruffly. "Why are you with them and not tied up? I didn't think you were a dumb Indian."

"Hmph!" Marty snorted, trying to think of a line to use to eat up time. "I didn't do anything wrong so why should I be tied up? No, these men were quite accommodating. We just did some trading and were finishing our breakfast when you showed up.

Oh," he added when he saw that one of the braves was ready to disarm Grant, "and they're not dumb."

The Young One rushed Grant, startling him, actually bewildering Rachel's nasty brother so much that he dropped his pistol without being hit. However, he still had a death grip on his knife, his metallic best friend, or at least the favorite part of his non-biological person. Nothing would make him give up his steely appendage.

Or, so he thought. The Young One was gone and now Number Two was in his face, glaring at him, fixing his intimidating gaze on a terrified Grant. Without batting an eye, Number Two kneed him in the groin, then forearmed him under the chin. He reached up and grabbed the knife as it went flying out of Grant's hand with the whiplash blow.

Red Shirt grunted and nodded at his men: tie him up. The worthless wad of white man was now lying sideways on the ground, his forehead bent into his knees, blubbering. He shamelessly wailed in pain, his voice high and squealing like a toddler who had just been robbed of his teddy bear. Number Two nudged Grant gruffly, not quite kicking him but definitely putting some force behind the foot. The groundling took the hint: stand up. Grant rolled onto his knees then stumbled upright, groaning in embarrassment as he noticed that he had pissed himself. He sniffed then groaned again. And shit himself, too.

Number Two grabbed Grant's right hand and wound a strip of rawhide around it, making a point to cinch it tightly. Grant pulled his left hand away, tucking it under his chin—he didn't want to be tied up. "I'll be good," he pled. "You don't need to tie me up."

Number Two grunted and nodded to the left hand: 'give it to me or else' was loud and clear in the guttural language of the victor.

"No, really—I promise…" Grant begged.

Twack! Number Two's fist found Grant's left jaw with a solid blow. Blood spurted out of the right side of his mouth with the impact. The pugilistic attitude adjustment knocked him sideways to the ground and his knees. A humbled Grant, still tethered to the Indian by the thong on his right wrist, stuck out his left hand. He cautiously lifted his head and, at the same time, moved his tongue around the inside of his mouth. His eyes opened wide—he found it. He spit out the tooth and grumbled, "It was rotten anyway."

Number Two quickly bound the whiner's left hand to his right then pushed the stinking, literally, whiner to the ground. Grant let out a groan as he landed on his butt—he was sitting in his own excrement. Red Shirt walked up to him and nudged his shoulder with his mocassined foot, letting his prisoner know that he was to lie back. Grant obeyed and looked up wide-eyed at the tall Indian. Red Shirt gently but firmly placed his foot on the man's throat and shook his head in admonishment. He was in command, not him, and he shouldn't have threatened him or his men, or tried to steal his horse. There would be repercussions. Grant sniffed and gulped but didn't say a word. Even if he had been dumb enough to try, it wouldn't have worked: the foot on his throat had paralyzed his larynx.

"No, they're not dumb," reiterated Marty. "They're actually very clever and I'm proud to claim them as friends. Now, where are your sister and the baby?"

"We're over here," called Rachel as she boldly walked up to the site of the confrontation. "I told you it was a stupid idea," she said angrily to her bloody-faced, sniveling brother. "You should have been happy with just the one horse. Serves you right though, for not letting us ride, too."

Red Shirt lifted his head to the man Marty figured was his second in command. At least he wasn't the youngest one who had acted as a waiter earlier. Number Two came over and took over the throat throttling position and Red Shirt sauntered over to Rachel.

The very young mother stood tall, unafraid on the outside, but trembling on the inside. He couldn't be any worse than her brothers. She let the red man touch the sleeve of her dress and caress the cheek of her son who was intrigued with the man with long black hair. Junior reached both arms out to Red Shirt, wanting to be held. The brave looked at Rachel to see how she felt about it—not that it would make any difference to him—she was a white woman. But, she wasn't like the other ones he had seen up close. They were all frantic at his sight, scared, screaming, and with water gushing out of their eyes and nose. No, she was different. Rachel dipped her head giving him tacit permission to hold her son.

Red Shirt took the child and saw right away he was different. She did not have the cloth on his behind to keep the wetness and filth next to his skin. She kept her son bare bottomed as he should be. She was young but had already proved to be healthy enough to produce a son. He nodded his head at her. Yes, he'd take her and the child with him.

"Wha, what are you going to do to me?" Grant whined pathetically. He had seen the Indian with the red shirt pawing his sister—he didn't care about that. He was afraid of what they were going to do to *him*. He'd heard the stories about what the Indians did to people who robbed, or tried to rob, them. The tales of torture flashed through his head as he screamed out again, "It was her idea—she told me to take the horse, and even gave me the gun!"

Red Shirt understood what the cowardly white man had said, but he could also see that he was lying. He looked back at the girl. She was shocked at his words and was now indignant. "You liar!" she shouted as she stomped toward his prone, panicked form. "You *took* that gun from me. No telling what you would have done to that poor man," she said pointing to Marty,

"If you had it then. He had less than we did! You took his horse and then you didn't even let him keep his boots! And you eat all the food, and make me walk, and, and…"

Rachel was frustrated beyond words so didn't even try to find them. "Asshole," she hissed, and then spat at him. She walked over to Red Shirt and her baby. "He's not worth it. Can we come with you?"

Red Shirt's eyes widened. This had to be a first: a white woman wanting to come live with a red man. He had planned to take her anyway, but she was willing, no, wanting to come with him. He shut his eyes and tipped his head, yes, and then gave her back her child. No, this was his child now. He had lost his wife and son last winter. These two would take their place. She was young and strong enough that she could bear him many more sons: and nice to look at, too. Today was a good day, a very good day.

8 Grant Gets His Due

Grant started blubbering again, "What are you going to do to me?" he pled. He tried to sniff back the tears and snot that were now streaking down his face like slug trails through dusty stones. "I'll be good, I promise," he begged again.

Marty saw the color of Red Shirt's face start to deepen. It was obvious he was fed up with the coward and wanted him to shut up. But, he also knew that the woman was related to him somehow, so didn't want to draw blood, or at least any more than Number Two had already brought forth with his quick, right cross to the jaw lesson in manners.

Marty spoke up both for and to him, "Grant, you might want to curb your tongue there before my friends decide that it might make a good pendant, eh?"

Grant gulped then subconsciously sucked in his lips, protecting what was inside. Cutting out tongues was one of the Indian tortures he had heard about. His pleas were falling on deaf ears anyway—these red men didn't speak English. Maybe they'd have pity on him because of the girl and his nephew. Yes, he'd give his sister to the Indian and the baby, too, for a while at least, and then maybe they'd let him go. "Eh, hem," Grant cleared his throat aloud, trying to get Red Shirt's attention.

He got it all right. Red Shirt walked purposely over to Grant, still lying obediently on his back, and glared at him. However, this time the Indian in charge did not put his foot on his prisoner's throat. He knew that he had the white intruder's complete attention and grinned as only a victor on the verge of causing extreme pain could. He would make this coward endure more of the same punishment he had used earlier for tormenting the woman. Red Shirt kicked dirt and gravel into Grant's face then backed away, issuing the order to his men: bury him.

The two braves scouted the area for wood and returned to Red Shirt with three pieces to use as the rough material for shovels. Number Two made short work of the timber with his hatchet, paring down a handle and flattening the other end for a spade. The Young One had found a suitable site and was removing the larger stones from the area, setting them in a pile for future use. Number Two handed a roughly hewn digger to both The Young One and Marty, then began digging.

Marty took the crude spade and worked just a fervently as the other two. He didn't know the exact details of Grant's punishment, or execution, but he knew that if he didn't help with the process, he might be stuck right next to him in the pit they were digging. He wasn't fond of Rachel's brother by any means, but these braves probably were going to make him suffer before they killed him outright. Grant might have a chance of survival if he was smart and strong... and could shut up. "Oh, well; too bad, so sad," he commented as he pulled out another shovelful. "Can't say he didn't deserve it."

Marty looked away from his task. He and the other two laborers had been working diligently and hadn't taken a break. It wasn't punishment for them, but wasn't an easy job either. Number Two grunted a short command that seemed to say, 'that's enough—let's stop for a drink.'

"Sounds good to me," Marty said aloud and followed the other two to the trees where Red Shirt, Rachel, and Junior were seated. Rachel was nursing her baby and chewing something at the same time. It appeared Red Shirt had given her some jerky for her breakfast.

Rachel picked up the canteen with her free hand, took a drink, and then smiled at her benefactor. He was a nice man and she hoped she would be able to stay with him. Grant had been telling her about New Bern and their cousin for four months at least. It was always two more days. She was beginning to doubt that there even was a relative in New Bern. However, she did know that New Bern was more than two days away. She wasn't trained in navigation; had never learned how to use the stars to guide her, but did know that they had passed the same areas several times on more than one occasion.

After they had lost their home, Grant didn't want to settle anywhere. All he wanted was to use her and her child to get sympathy and food—or to use as a distraction while he pillaged and robbed. She knew he did that whenever he found the opportunity. She knew it was bad, but there was nothing she could do about it. She had asked him to stop on two different occasions. In retrospect, she should have bit her tongue after the first thrashing he had given her for sassing him. No, he wouldn't listen to reason and had no scruples. The worst part though, was that he never shared his spoils with her or the baby. She shook her head to erase the bad memories of him and their brother, Atholl, Senior, her child's father. She looked back at Red Shirt and smiled in relief. Even if this man was an enemy, at least he gave her food.

He didn't like to hurt people. There had been too much of it in his short life, but this man needed to be taught a lesson, even if by one not of his family or tribe. He had seen the man be cruel to the horse and, just as bad, the woman and child. He couldn't just let him go—that would be a sign of weakness in front of his men. Killing him swiftly would be easiest, but burying him up to his neck with rocks and dirt would be a fair punishment, too. If he did manage to get out of his earthen grave, he would probably be so weak that he wouldn't be able to make it to water. There weren't many creeks or streams around here and the few springs in the area well hidden. Yes, he'd let his men bury him then let the woman throw on the last shovelful of dirt, if she wished. She didn't seem to care for him even though they had been traveling together.

Red Shirt grunted his order; this time using several words of his Indian language. He pointed at Marty and signed for him to help the other two. The three were to assist Grant to his tomb of shame. Of course, Grant wasn't too eager to go. He kicked and wriggled like a live fish on a hot frying pan, squealing and whining that it wasn't his fault. "It was her that did it. She told me to take the stallion, that the mare wasn't good enough for her. She gave me the gun and said to shoot the damned Indians. The only good Injun was a dead one. She, she ..."

Twack! This time Red Shirt took the honor of shutting off the free flowing faucet of lies. He shook his head and snorted at the pathetic excuse for a man: white, red or otherwise. He not only lied, he was blaming a woman, a woman of his own family who he had abused, for his wrongdoings.

Grant was stunned but still conscious. He tried to open his mouth to protest, but his face wouldn't respond. He brought his bound hands up under his chin and realized why he couldn't speak: his mouth was open all the way and he couldn't close or move it. His jaw was either broken or dislocated. He looked to Rachel, pleading with his eyes since his voice wouldn't work. He could see that she didn't care though. No, wait—she did care. She was smirking and shaking her head side to side, relishing his predicament.

"How do *you* like being hit in the face? Not very nice, eh?" she remarked then snorted in disgust. She had zero sympathy for the brother who beat her for sport, let her have just enough food to live, and wiped his ass with her hat. "Let the devil have you then," she said then walked away from the pit. They could do what they wanted to him.

As it turned out, the ground was too hard and the implements too primitive to dig a proper man-sized pit. They settled for a grave that was deeper at one end than the other.

Inevitably, Number Two had to hit Grant one last time to knock him unconscious. Even binding his legs hadn't helped much. His wiggle potential was too high for the three of them and Red Shirt didn't want to stoop to the level of enforcer and assist in the punishment.

The braves each carried a leg. Marty supported the shoulder and lax head, which flopped to the left, the jaw, set catty-wumpus to the right. Just as they were getting ready to drop him into the pit, Marty hollered, "My boots! Can I get my boots back, please?" His hands and arms were full of passed out male so he couldn't employ his usual sign language to communicate his message, but still managed to nod to the feet. "He stole those from me. His were in the saddlebag. They might be there still…"

Marty looked up at Number Two to see if he understood. He did all right. He was grinning. He nodded down to his own feet. Marty hadn't noticed earlier, but Number Two was wearing Grant's old boots. "Then can I have mine back? I mean, they probably wouldn't fit you anyway. I have big feet."

Number Two looked over to Red Shirt to verify that it was okay. Red Shirt gave his now familiar grunt of assent so the three men stepped back and put the shit-smelling body back down. Marty scrambled to the opposite end and tugged. The boots, too big for Grant, came off easily. He unzipped them and stuck his bare feet inside, quickly zipping them up without his missing socks. "Thanks, mates," Marty said then went back to his shoulder toting position, ready for the other two to grab their end.

So, Marty had his boots back and Grant, the mean big brother, thief, liar, and general black-hearted creature, was laid out in a relatively shallow grave, buried up to his neck in dirt. The tomb was secured by various sizes of boulders to deter, or at least slow down, egress by him or access by coyotes, foxes, or wolves. The ants weren't out, not even butterflies were flying about. No, the little six-legged critters like flies, ants, and wasps wouldn't bother him. But, the four-legged kind would be attracted to the smell of blood from his earlier thrashing. They might not be able to get to the main course of limbs and torso, but they *could* snack on the tender bits like his nose, ears, and eyeballs. He'd be lucky if he died of thirst before they found him.

Then, Red Shirt did something odd. At first Marty didn't know if it was cruel or kind. The chief dribbled water into Grant's mouth. The wetness revived him and probably slaked his thirst a bit. His mouth started to work right; he could smack his lips, so Red Shirt poured some more down his gullet. Yes, it was cruel. Now Grant was alert and probably had an extra twenty-four hours of torment before he passed out from thirst or died. It was midmorning and not too hot, but there were lots of daylight hours left.

The Young One and Number Two were already mounted and waiting for orders. Red Shirt looked to Rachel; made sure he had her attention, and then lifted the makeshift shovel, offering her a chance to throw on the last bit of dirt and gravel. Rachel frowned, shook her head, and then turned her back on her brother. She was done with Grant and didn't want anything more to do with him, either in anger or in kindness. He was nothing to her now.

"Well," Marty started, not really knowing what he was going to say. He had to think of something though. He didn't want to stay where he was and had already been lost when the Indians found him. "Which way are we going?" he asked, finding a neutral, he hoped, topic.

Red Shirt looked him in the eye then canted his head toward the others: 'You're welcome to join us,' he said with his easy to understand body language.

"Thanks, don't mind if I do," Marty said loudly, trying to drown out the protests coming from the misaligned mouth of the newly interred.

"Wait..oo canna gaw wid aut me," Grant mumbled.

"You can't go without me?" Marty translated. "Oh, but I can. Oh, and I gave the horse you stole from me to my new friends here and managed to get my boots back. Paybacks a bitch, dude!" Marty crowed then looked to the others.

Red Shirt was lifting Rachel and the baby onto Marty's former mare and the others were already riding away. Marty bent down, picked up a piece of the wood cut from the improvised shovel, and stuck it in Grant's mouth. "Use it well and you might get yourself out," he instructed. "Worked for Owen Wilson in 'Shanghai Noon.' It might work for you, too, if you use your lips for something besides complaining."

9 Rachel Rides to Freedom

They still hadn't traveled far enough away—she could still hear him. "Hmm, hmm, hmm, hmm," Rachel hummed, her tune with no name getting louder as her brother's pathetic begging increased, his pleas more annoying than entreating. He'd had many chances over the years to be a good person. Every time they got food, he'd only give her his leftovers. If there was a blanket, he'd take it, not even letting her lie near him to benefit from his warmth. He'd whip her for not walking fast enough, talking too much, not cooking dinner to his satisfaction, or just because, he said, 'he felt like it.' No, Grant was nothing to her now.

Red Shirt had let her and the baby ride the horse. She knew she was on the mare Grant stole from the man who was now walking behind her. It didn't seem to bother him that he was afoot while she was riding his horse though. She smiled as she recalled how he had made the joke about eating fish for breakfast, lunch, dinner, and dessert. Too bad she couldn't give him back his hat, and the hook and line. Grant had thrown them in the fire, saying he was cold and didn't want to get up for more wood. Besides, he complained, it looked stupid on her. But, she knew the real reason: he didn't want her to have anything, even a man's hat that was too big for her head.

As if he had been reading her mind, the man trotted up beside her. "What happened to your hat? It sure looked cute on you," Marty said, feeling braver now that her brother's knife wasn't flashing in his face.

Rachel shrugged and said much with her one word, "Grant," then rolled her eyes with disgust. She didn't want to recall anything about him. He was from her past life.

"Well, Rachel, it seems we haven't been properly introduced. I'm Marty Melbourne and I was trying to find my way home when I got, um, disoriented." Marty could tell she didn't want to remember events that pertained to her dastardly brother, so he skipped the episode that referred to his being robbed. She already knew that part anyhow. "These kind men and I did some trading, then they fed me, gave me water to drink, and we did a bit of talking, sort of. I think Red Shirt knows where I need to go, but I'm not too sure he wants to lead me there. Did he say anything to you?"

Rachel shook her head. She liked Marty but really didn't have any news for him.

"Did he tell you where we were headed?" he asked. She shook her head again. He should know that she didn't speak Indian and Red Shirt didn't speak English.

"Well, at least I'll have you to talk to," Marty said then chuckled. In the course of their short conversation, she had only said one word, "Grant," and he knew she didn't want to say that again. For right now though, he didn't have anything else to say. Time would tell where they were headed. At least they were traveling as a little tribe and not as conquerors and hostages.

After a couple of hours, Red Shirt raised his arm to signal that they would stop for a break. The Young One handed out more jerky and the canteen was passed around afterwards. One at a time, the men walked away from the group then came back. Well, Marty decided he needed a potty break, too. When he returned, he realized that Rachel was still standing, rocking her baby back and forth in her arms. "If you'd like to, um, take a break, I'll hold the baby for you," Marty offered then canted his head over to a stand of bushes that would afford her some privacy for her toilet.

Rachel took him up on the offer, ceding her progeny to the silly man dressed in a long blue shirt, leather breechclout, and boots that came half way up his shins. "Thanks," she said, then scurried away to do her business.

Marty graciously took the boy, happy to hold a surrogate for the son he hoped to see soon, very soon. "So what's your name, little boy?" he asked comically, crossing his eyes and speaking in a high voice to get a giggle out of the lad. The little boy, he estimated he was about a year old, chuckled heartily. He had performed the same antics for James when he was a baby and got the same results. "Works every time," he commented softly.

"Mine," Red Shirt said gruffly as he strode up purposely and took the boy out of Marty's arms, holding him possessively, close to his chest.

"Okay," Marty said with a shadow of fear in his voice. It wasn't the word, but how he had said it. Then he realized that it *was* the word, too. "Mine? You speak English?" Marty asked, stunned as he realized that he must.

Red Shirt didn't answer but instead turned away from Marty and took over the infantile conversation, babbling incoherently to the boy.

Rachel came back and saw her baby had been exchanged between the two men then saw the shocked look on Marty's face. "Did I miss something?" she asked sincerely.

Red Shirt ignored her so Marty volunteered the answer. "Red Shirt laid claim to Junior there. He said 'mine' and took him. It looks like the lad has a real Pa now."

Rachel beamed but didn't say a word. Instead, she walked up to Red Shirt; his back was still to her and Marty, and put her arm through his, joining him in holding her son, their son. Red Shirt didn't say anything but pulled his shoulders back in pride. He had a wife and heir now.

The Indian band with their two new members and one tag-along continued down the unmarked trail to wherever it was they were going. Marty wanted to be on his way to his own home but didn't want to be lost again. He'd go with the Indians for now. He was sure Red Shirt knew where The Trees were. It may be that he first had to get his men and new family back to his village or settlement or whatever it was called, but hopefully, after they were all safely ensconced, he'd see fit to show him the way to The Trees.

The sun was getting low and no village was in sight. However, Marty could smell water—there was a creek nearby. They made the last half-mile at a quickened pace. The horses were trotting and he was jogging, but he knew why. If they got to the creek at the right time, they'd have fresh fish for supper. The jerky provided sustenance but wasn't a belly filler.

Number Two and The Young One picked up the pace and raced ahead. As they sped ahead, Red Shirt slowed his pace, coming in front of Rachel's horse to bring her back to an easy walk. He'd let his men catch dinner and start the fire so all was ready for him, his new family, and crazy white man friend when they got there.

And, so it was. In the half hour that it took for the late shift to catch up with the hospitality crew, dinner and a fire were waiting. Red Shirt took his son from Rachel, offering her his free hand to help her dismount. She accepted it graciously and gave him a sincere smile of gratitude that promised more, hopefully. He wanted to lie with her tonight. It would be best if he sealed the union before they got back to the village.

"That's some mighty fine fare you fixed there, men," Marty commented after finishing his filet of trout on a stick. "I'd offer to wash the dishes but since we didn't have any, I'd like to know if anyone would mind if I went down to the creek and washed myself up a bit." Marty stuck his nose near his armpit and sniffed, made an ugly face, then grinned at his small audience.

Red Shirt was standing close to Rachel, who was seated, feeding little bits of trout to her son. He nodded and grinned:

'That's a good idea, stinky white man—go,' he said without words.

Marty trundled down to the creek and found a shallow, calm pool. The water wasn't warm but wasn't icy like the fast moving stream either. He took off his boots and set them on a boulder. He removed his malodorous shirt and tossed it into the still pond. Now, his Indian wear: the breechclout. This time he knew what he was doing. He untied the knot and pulled away the thong, bowed his legs like Red Shirt had, and let the leather loincloth drop to the dry ground. It didn't need cleaning but he did. Marty picked his way over the slippery, moss covered river rocks, sat down in the tepid pool, and employed fistfuls of sand as his soapy washcloth. He scrubbed the stink of two weeks of sweat and dust off his skin, bent his head sideways, and sniffed his armpit: fresh as a North Carolina mountain stream. He reached over and rubbed the shirt into the sand at the bottom of the small pond. Fish poop smell would be better than marinated man odor. He finished his primeval bath with a silica face and scalp scrub. "Too bad the whiskers won't rub off," he commented as he ran the back of his index finger over his scraggly beard. "But, at least there's no chance of lice now."

Marty rinsed his shirt a second time, twisted and wrung it out as best he could, then shook it briskly a dozen times, flipping out as many of the residual drops of creek water as he could. He threw it over his shoulder and exited his bath, taking deep cleansing breaths, trying to keep his newfound confidence in place. He didn't know where he was going or what was waiting for him at the end of the journey. He'd have to wait to go home to his own family, but at least he now had a better chance of finding the right route; Red Shirt could help him as long as he stayed in his good graces. He bit his bottom lip then bent over and retrieved his thong belt and breechclout, slipping it on in, for him, record time. 'I can be a good red white man,' he thought. 'At least I don't have to put on an act. Red Shirt likes me as I am.'

"I think I'll let you dry out a bit," he said aloud to his shirt as he spread it out over a bush at the edge of the creek. Marty picked up his boots and walked back slowly toward the campfire, using its glow as his beacon. He carried his boots rather than wear them for the short walk back. His feet were damp and his boots still stank of Grant. He'd bear the discomfort of walking over sharp stones for a few yards in exchange for having dry tootsies and aired out footwear for the morrow.

The sleeping arrangements were already established. Number Two was at the end of camp where they had come in and The Young One was at the other end, the two sentries positioned at the most logical entrances. Red Shirt was sitting next to Rachel, who was nursing Junior, evidently giving him his bedtime nightcap. Red Shirt looked up at Marty, held his gaze, and shifted his eyes away from the fire, back to where Marty had just come from. 'We want to be alone tonight: sleep over there,' he said without words.

"Good night, everyone; I'll be sleeping down there if you need me for anything," Marty commented to the air above the three of them. He realized it was perfunctory—the new little family had everything they needed in each other.

Red Shirt watched as Rachel discreetly bared her breast to feed her son. She looked up, saw him watching her, and pulled the blouse down further, exposing more of her skin to his view. Marty was gone and so were the two other braves. It was just her, the baby, and the man who she had chosen as his father. No, not just his father—this was the man she wanted as her husband.

She had thought that all men were pigs. At least the ones she had known growing up were. Her father and Atholl had been fondling and clutching at her since she could remember. It wasn't until she had sneaked into Sunday school one trip into town that she realized that what they did was wrong. She hadn't heard the whole story the preacher was telling: Grant had reached in and yanked her away before the sermon was over, but she had heard enough. A man was not to touch a woman who was not his wife. She tried telling her father what the preacher had said, but he slapped her and told her the man was lying.

A short time later, her father was dead. He had cut his hand while butchering the hog. The wound had festered, become red and hot all the way up to his shoulder, over the next two days. She had tried to tend to it, but he wouldn't let her touch him. He screamed all that night in pain, cursing and crying. She had slept with the goats to keep away from the noise. When she came back to the house the next morning, he was quiet, very quiet. He was also dead.

She felt sorry for him, sort of, but she couldn't have done anything. The day before he died, he made Atholl promise to take care of her, take care of her real good. "Don't let her get wayward or get big ideas in her head. Don't let her talk to the other women or go to Church. Smack her if she gets out of line, and give her the strap every once in a while, 'just because.' She doesn't need much so don't give it to her."

Well, Atholl had done what Daddy had said and was happy to take over 'the good part of havin' a daughter.' However, Atholl did more than grab and paw; he wanted more. The first time he did it, he had given her whisky until she passed out. She woke up with him on top of her, sweating and panting. Then he collapsed on her chest, almost suffocating her. The next morning, he was gone and she hurt; hurt real bad between her legs and behind her eyes. She knew what the pain between her legs was and didn't tell him about that. The pain in the head was a hangover, he said. "I guess you won't be getting any more whisky," he told her. "I'll not waste it on you if it's just going to make you sick."

Then for the next few weeks, he'd wait until she was asleep before he came in and 'did his duty.' Later, he got braver, not even bothering to wait until she was asleep. She tried hiding in the woods in the evening to escape his attentions, hoping that he'd be *asleep when she returned. She didn't want to come home to the strap and his drunken pawing and caressing that inevitably led to him shoving her down and pulling up her shift, putting his stinky prick between her legs. She gave up crying when he did it because he seemed to like it when she did. "Come on, give me some more tears," he'd holler, and then smack her cheek. "I like it when you move around like a worm on a rock."*

When her belly started swelling and she felt movement, she realized she was pregnant. She had watched the cat have her kittens and figured out how to pant and breathe when it was time for babies to come. She birthed the first baby, her daughter, by herself. She was proud of her effort; the child was so perfect. She also became bolder. When Atholl came to her a week later to 'do his duty,' she told him, no; she didn't want him near her again. She had already decided that she was leaving but didn't tell him that. She would find a way to escape him and Grant and make a better life for her and her daughter. He glared at her when she said 'no,' grabbed his bottle of whisky, and left for the barn.

She went back to work in the kitchen. A couple hours later, she left little Esther napping in the house while she went outside to gather eggs. Her daughter was still asleep when she got back. She was sleeping longer than usual though, she was usually hungry every couple of hours. Something didn't seem right so she woke her. Or tried to. When she picked her up, the little blanket fell away and she saw the bloody clout and gown. She had spurned Atholl so he 'did his duty' to her infant daughter and killed her, battering her insides, and causing her to bleed to death.

She buried the baby wrapped in the only thing she could, the bloody shroud she had found her in. There wasn't even wood for a proper casket. She dug a deep grave; made sure she piled lots of rocks on top of it, and pulled up nearby wild flowers, transplanting them at the head of the site. Little Esther would have fresh flowers for eternity.

After the internment, she grabbed a half loaf of bread, her blanket, a jug of water, and walked away. She wouldn't have left them a note even if she had paper, quill and ink, and had known how to write. She was done with Atholl and Grant.

Or so she thought. She had only been gone one day when they found her asleep, just outside of town. Atholl and Grant took turns whipping her, 'Just to make sure she got the message.' She never tried to leave again.

Atholl took her whenever he had the drink. She didn't try to resist anymore. But, she did hide his whisky. He wouldn't even look at her 'that way' when he was sober. He didn't have the urge unless he was drunk. A short time later, he left 'to do his soldiering' and was gone for months at a time, sparing her his attentions.

At least Grant didn't touch her 'that way.' She had never seen the results of Daddy's wrath but had overheard Atholl teasing him on several occasions. 'Little no prick' he called him. "Still sittin' down to piss?" he'd taunt when Grant went to the privy. "Daddy's first daughter," he'd crow, then laugh until Grant was so red in the face, she thought he'd burst. They had fought a few times when the teasing was too much for Grant, but Atholl was much bigger and older. He'd thrash him every time. After Grant was beat, he'd find her, whipping her to vent his frustration at losing the fight with his big brother, or as he said, "Just because."

Atholl had wanted to be a real soldier, had even managed to steal an officer's uniform, but the British army didn't want him. "Too much anger," they said.

"How could a soldier have too much anger," he carped. "They need captains like me to get the soldiers inspired. Kill 'em all! Kill all the Colonists and take their money and livestock. Americans my ass—they're just a bunch of cattle that need to be watched over and harvested."

No, it wasn't until she had seen Evie and Wallace together that she knew there was another way for a man and a woman to be together. Sarah had found her and Grant on the road to New Bern and invited them to take a break and share a meal with her. She was a healer and wanted to check on her and her babies: Junior, the one young 'un she was toting on her shoulder, and the one still in her womb. Yes, Sarah probably saved her life three months ago by delivering her of her dead infant daughter, Mary.

Sarah and Evie may have saved her life but they definitely saved her sanity. They told her of hope—that she could have a new life with Junior. They said they were sure she could find a good man but to make sure she was married to him before she gave him children. Well, Red Shirt was a good man. He was also an Indian. She didn't know how they performed a marriage. Maybe taking care of her, feeding her, and letting her ride the horse was part of their ritual. She nodded. Even if it weren't, she'd believe it was. She wanted to be married to him.

She had watched the way Wallace had sex with—no, he made love to, Evie. They didn't know she was watching; she pretended to be asleep. She heard the soft words of love. "I love making love to my wife," he had said, then kissed her all over. The moaning Evie made wasn't of pain. She was enjoying it more than eating fresh baked apple pie with cream. At the end, she heard both of them panting. Both of them! She knew Atholl panted when he was finished, or almost finished, but Evie did, too. Maybe some women got that same feeling that made Atholl grin so big when he was done and made her all sticky. At least she knew Evie was extra happy the next morning and didn't appear to be hurting.

Red Shirt watched as she wrapped the sleeping boy in the blanket and lay him down beside her. She left her breast bared then turned to him. He tried to control his breathing but kept gulping air as she removed her blouse. She stood up slowly and untied the strings that held her clothing around her waist. She let her skirt drop then looked at him and smiled. She bent over and pushed the clothing into a makeshift bed then sat down on top of it. She put her hands out in invitation.

As she was undressing, he had noticed the lash marks on the back of her legs where she had been whipped. She couldn't have done that to herself—the thief he had buried this morning must have done it to her. No wonder she didn't care about him. Yes, her legs and back were marked but the rest of her was perfect. She was pale and a bit bony but her breasts were round and full and her hips were wide enough to bear children. And, she wanted him.

Red Shirt stood up. He hoped he wouldn't have trouble getting the white man's pants off. His manhood had swelled and was uncomfortably bent behind the buttons. He didn't want to embarrass himself with being awkward in undressing as he came to her as her husband for the first time, but these white man's pants weren't as easy to remove as his breechclout.

Rachel saw that Red Shirt was having difficulty in unbuttoning his pants. She wasn't sure if it was because of his excited condition or if he was just new to brass buttons. The other braves were wearing breechclouts, as was Marty. Marty had said they did some trading. This had to be it: Red Shirt had traded 'pants' with Marty.

Rather than shame him by exposing his clumsiness, Rachel decided to make the undressing a part of the lovemaking. At least she remembered that Wallace and Evie had shared the task, so maybe the red man did, too. She stood up, moved in close to Red Shirt, and put her hands around his waist, gently stroking his back. She slowly worked her hands around to the front of him and stroked the front of his pants, eliciting a gasp from him as she touched his firmness. She smiled at him and tip toed up to give him a gentle kiss on the lips, making sure she left her hands on the waistband of his pants. The kiss lasted longer than she thought it would and that was fine by her. She had never been kissed, really.

Her father and her brother had forced their mouths on hers but those weren't kisses. What she was getting from Red Shirt felt great!

She stroked her hand down the outside front of his fly again. She carefully put the fingertips of one hand inside the top of his pants while unbuttoning with the other. She slowly worked her way down, unbuttoning one brass stud at a time until the access was open. She reached in, wrapped her fingers around his hard cock, and freed it from its awkward angle inside the cotton cloth. It sprung up of its own accord next to his belly, hot and pulsing, eager to mate.

Rachel wasn't sure what she should do next. Surely, the Indians had their own way to make love. She'd let him take over. She was pretty sure, no, she was positive, that whatever he was going to do it wouldn't be done in anger or with cruelty.

She wanted him. Even his wife hadn't been so generous in her kisses and caresses. She had seen his predicament and taken care of the closures on his new pants, freeing his manhood and letting him know that she would take him as a husband. Now she was on the ground, waiting for him to make the next move. Yes, he would join with her and make her his wife. His hands were on his hips, ready to shove his pants down, when he remembered Dances Naked's advice: take off your moccasins first. He bent over quickly and untied his laces, stepping on the toes to remove his footwear swiftly and efficiently. Now it was time for the best part. He shimmied out of the white man's pants and stepped over to his bride, straddling her now prone position. Maybe his seed would overtake hers and he'd make a baby on the first try. But, even if it didn't, he'd keep making happy with her. Daylight was a long ways away.

10 There Once Was a Village
August 21, 1781

Breakfast for the group consisted of cold water consumed in a reserved silence. The two braves had already removed traces of their campfire by the time Marty was back from his toilet—they were ready to roll.

Red Shirt helped his new wife and son onto the mare, both unable and unwilling to hold his pride in check. He didn't have to tell his men that this was his woman now—they could see it in his face. Number Two would be back with his wife soon and The Young One still had a winter or two until he would be ready for a mate. Maybe he'd help Dances Naked get back to his woman and maybe he wouldn't. That was a bad medicine area and he didn't need any more problems. His tribe was still trying to recover from the terrors of the last two years.

Red Shirt set a respectable pace for their journey. They could have moved faster, but the white man was old and on foot. If he didn't like him, he would have traveled faster to get to his home and not cared whether the man could keep up with them or became lost again. But, this man had done him no wrong and seemed to be on good terms with his new wife. He also helped subdue and punish the bad man, not arguing whether it was wrong or cruel to do so. Yes, Dances Naked was smart and obedient. If he weren't so old, he'd make a good brave, regardless of whether he was red or white.

Marty could tell they were getting close to their destination. The men's postures were changing, their backs now straight and vigilant. Their eyes darted quickly, surveying the surrounding brush and trees as if they were on the lookout for someone watching them. They were on sentry alert. Something was wrong here though. Shoot, he'd be happier than Christmas morning to be back to his home. These men didn't seem to be sure of what they were riding into.

As it turned out, no one greeted the group. Red Shirt dismounted and signaled to the rest of his band to stay mounted—they might have to leave soon.

A bent over old woman with a tall walking stick, and even taller attitude, came out from a cobbled together hovel of brush and hides, commanding everyone's respect with her deportment. Red Shirt listened to her questions but didn't reply with words, only grunted. Marty knew that sound: he was pretty good at picking up on his new companion's guttural emanations. "I'll handle these people—don't worry about them," he seemed to say without using his words, English or Cherokee.

However, Old Woman didn't believe him; or maybe she just didn't trust him to be capable. Either way, her determined scowl and labored walk over to the new people in the village was an insult to Red Shirt. Marty saw the way his offended companion sucked in his breath, deciding it was better to keep quiet than create a row. He pulled back his shoulders and waited for Old Woman to verify what he had just told her was true: these white people were harmless.

Old Woman came to within six feet of Marty and stopped. She pointed at him with her carved walking stick, saying words he didn't understand. Her body language wasn't readable. All he could tell was that she was ticked off. She walked a few feet closer then prodded his belly with the earthen end of her cane. He still didn't understand her words except that they were the same ones repeated over and over again. Her actions weren't any clearer either. She nudged him again, this time harder and more insistent, with the same gruff, unintelligible command. Marty looked over to Red Shirt for guidance and saw him subtly touch his own shirt: 'pull up your shirt.'

"Yes, ma'am," Marty said politely and pulled up his long, blue shirt, completely exposing his breechclout and belly. He looked around and saw that several other old women had come out from behind the makeshift shelter and were now watching the physical examination. He looked down at his torso again and realized why she was so concerned. "No, ma'am; I don't have the measles. See," he said as he pulled his shirt off over his head then raised his arms so she could see his armpits, turning to show his back, "no redness and, if you care to touch me, you'll see I have no fever. She and the baby are fine, too," he said as he pointed to Rachel. "No sickness," he mimed fatigue and put the back of his hand up to his forehead as if to check for fever. "None," he said and shook his head.

Marty perked back up to his healthy, white man persona, "We're all good," he said with a smile and started to put his shirt back on.

"Blah, blah, blah, blah-blah," said Old Woman as she walked toward Rachel's horse, doggedly stabbing the ground with her walking stick with each step. She was not a happy person and not satisfied with Red Shirt's explanation.

Red Shirt took long, broad steps, almost ran, to his new family. Marty could see the reserve he was using. If he ran, it could be seen as a sign of weakness. He stood by Rachel's side, resolute, his arms crossed in front of his chest, preventing Old Woman from starting her examination. Marty didn't know the words he used but the meaning was clear to him and to Rachel: 'This is my woman and I will take care of her. Do not touch her—she's clean.' Red Shirt dismissed the crone with a nod then took the reins from Rachel and headed away from the belligerent old woman and her coterie.

"Good day, ma'am," Marty said to the matriarch then made a hop, step, long stride movement, not quite a run, to catch up with Red Shirt, Rachel, and the baby. He didn't know where they were going, but he definitely felt more comfortable with his new clan than the one, wary old biddy, and her big stick.

Evidently, their group had passed the medical examination. Number Two and The Young One, who hadn't been interrogated or examined, followed behind them to the separate little encampment a few hundred yards beyond the first site. A young girl, Marty figured she was six or seven, was toting a crying baby. Actually, the lass was crying just as much if not more than the baby. Number Two jumped off his horse when he saw her and grabbed and held both of them to his chest. He listened to her words then he, too, was wailing.

"Rachel," Marty called as he walked up to her, still mounted on the mare. "Give Junior to Red Shirt or me, then go see if you can take care of that little baby. I think Number Two's wife died and those are his children. I don't see anyone around here other than you who looks like she's equipped to see to the wee'un's needs."

"Huh?" Rachel asked as she handed Junior to Marty in an act of faith and family.

"Go nurse the babe, will you?" he said plainly, canting his head to the wailing trio then helping her down.

Rachel walked up cautiously to the distressed family. She wasn't sure how to communicate her desire to help them then realized she'd just show them what she was offering. She untied her blouse and bared her breast, putting out both arms to the father who was now holding his baby. 'Let me help,' she said without words.

Number Two had seen this woman feed her son. He knew she had milk. Yes, she was now his brother-in-law's wife but she was still a white woman. If she gave her milk to his son, he'd be part white man, too. He looked down and saw his son, still crying but without as much energy as a young one should when distressed. Yes, he'd rather have his son part white than dead. He lifted his head and ceded his son to her, 'Here, please help; I appreciate it,' was his heartfelt, unspoken message.

Little One rubbed his nose back and forth on the nipple. It wasn't the same smell as his mother but it was milk and not the coarse mixture that Big Sister had been urging him to eat. He nursed heartily, letting the new mother pull him away after a few minutes to rub his back. He gave her a long, loud burp then nuzzled his head back down toward her breast—he wasn't finished yet.

Red Shirt stood away from the group, assessing the situation without interfering. Marty walked over to him and spoke softly, "Looks like the measles got to your tribe here. Is that what happened to your other family?" he asked.

Red Shirt cut his eyes to him and shut them slowly in a tacit, affirmative answer, then opened them back up and watched Rachel feed his nephew. Now his sister was dead, too. He had always loved his sister, she was his twin, and he wanted to cry and wail as his brother-in-law had, but he needed to be strong. He thought that the red belly disease was gone but it had come back. His father had over fifty braves in this tribe two years ago. Now he was dead and there were only three braves left including him. They hadn't been successful in the hunt and winter was coming. He still had to see to the needs of the old ones and the children first. He snorted in disgust. There weren't many that he had to feed, but he still had nothing. He looked over at Marty. And now he had the white man to feed, too.

Marty had seen the look that Red Shirt gave him. To him he was just another mouth to feed. And, by the looks of everyone's leanness, there wasn't much food to share. There had to be a way that he could help these people.

"If there's a town nearby, I have some money. Maybe I could buy some bacon or cornmeal or well, whatever I have is yours. You helped me and I'd like to return the favor. But, I think that I should be the one to do the purchasing. That is, I should be the one to go to the store. I don't think the white man, the other white men, would be fair to an Indian with the value of the money. That and they probably wouldn't believe that I just 'gave' you money. Some of those white folks are pretty nasty. But you know that already, don't you?"

Red Shirt snorted in agreement. He didn't understand everything Dances Naked had said, but he was pretty sure that he was offering to buy food for his people and to beware of white men. All he needed was to be shown the way to a store or trading post.

"Sound like a plan?" Marty asked. He saw the confused, uncertain look on Red Shirt's face then realized he was using 21st century jargon. Think 18th century, Melbourne! "Take me to the white man's town and I'll buy food and give it to you."

Red Shirt lifted his head; he understood. He looked hard at Marty; he knew that there must be more. Dances Naked wanted something for this.

"Yes, I want something," Marty answered the unspoken question. "When we come back with the food and after you make sure that your clan or family or tribe or…sorry; I'm babbling." Marty straightened his back and started again, employing more hand language. He shifted Junior to his hip and opened his one available arm toward Red Shirt then brought it back to himself. "I want to help you and would like for you to help me. I'll buy food for your family, but I want you to help me get back to mine." Marty ended his statement of terms with the single-handed air drawing of a curvy woman, bringing his cupped hand to his heart to make sure he knew he was speaking of his woman. He looked down at Junior once again, this time seeing in him his missing son, his eyes leaking tears as he recalled his dilemma. Red Shirt was back with his family—he wanted his, too.

Red Shirt looked back to Rachel and his nephew. His arms suddenly felt so empty. He grunted and Marty knew why: give him his son. "Here's your boy," he said. "So, do we wait for tomorrow? I mean," Marty tipped his head sideways and shut his eyes like he was sleeping then opened them again, "do we go in the morning after we've had a good night's sleep?" he asked hopefully.

Red Shirt gave a heartfelt chuckle and smiled as he nodded. 'Yes, they'd leave in the morning.' This white man was funny and generous. He must be part Indian. Or crazy.

The young girl, Marty called her Big Sister, made a cornmeal gruel and set it out for everyone to share, making sure that the men had as much as they wanted before she came back for the bowl. Red Shirt had kept hold of Junior and used his finger to bring the viscous blend to the lad's mouth. Evidently, the food agreed with him because he kept hold of the digit and gnawed on it afterwards, trying to get the last bit of corn off it. Either that or the boy was teething. He seemed to be that age, Marty recalled.

Red Shirt offered the dinner in a dish to his niece. She brought the half-empty bowl over to Rachel and the two of them used their fingers to lick the bowl clean. Marty had wanted more and he knew that the other men did, too. They were all hungry, but they had eaten fish the night before. The little girl probably hadn't had much to eat and Rachel was nursing two babies. She deserved a larger share, too.

Rachel was enchanted with the young girl. Marty could see the tenderness in her eyes as she watched the girl bring more wood to the fireside. He theorized that if she and Grant were their only family, she had probably never had a little sister. That and she had a son; she probably wanted a daughter, too. Well, after the way she and Red Shirt had been going at it nearly all night the night before, she'd be with child soon. Hmph! No wonder Red Shirt didn't want to leave to guide him to The Trees: he was still a newlywed. Their accommodations for a honeymoon didn't seem to bother them last night. Tonight looked like they'd have a bit more privacy, but he might have to share her attentions. She had a new mouth to feed.

Yes, it looked like the little brave would live now. He hadn't seen any milk goats or cows around, and infants didn't do well on corn gruel. As strange as the last 36 hours had been, it looked like this eclectic collection of people was meant to be in each other's lives. God knew what he was doing. They were all fulfilling each other's needs.

11 The Shopping Trip
August 22, 1781

Marty made himself useful after dinner and helped Big Sister gather wood. He felt like the odd man out in this tribe. Shoot, he was the odd man! No home, no designated job or tasks, no family, he didn't speak their language, wasn't used to their pasty food... but he did have *something* in common with them: his butt flap. Red Shirt was still wearing the pants they had traded for. Marty noticed him a few times discretely grabbing his crotch to rearrange his man parts. Well, he'd wait until it was just the two of them and tell the red man that he'd be a lot more comfortable if he tucked in his shirt and used the softer cotton cloth as a barrier to the rough denim. Marty wiggled as he thought about it. The soft leather breechclout really was comfortable and non-restrictive. 'Hmm,' he wondered, 'I wonder if I could get away with wearing this when I go back home? Nah, at least not in public. However, he realized as he thought about it more, Bibb might find an Indian buck running around in nothing but a thong and a panel of tanned deer hide, quite provocative. "Stop it," he told himself aloud. "No fantasizing until bedtime."

Big Sister looked over at the crazy white man to see if something was wrong. Her uncle had told her not to fear him, but to make sure he didn't do anything to hurt himself: he would be useful to the tribe. She trusted her uncle, but this animal with two legs didn't look like any man she had ever seen. The top half looked almost like a white man, bearded and with curly hair, but most white men wore a hat: he was bare headed like an Indian.

96

The middle part looked Indian, too. She was pretty sure that Dances Naked was wearing Red Shirt's breechclout, but she could be wrong—she never looked that closely at a man's clothing. And then, there was the bottom part: bony white legs with footwear that looked different from any she had seen. Those weren't moccasins nor were they the black shoes with buckles like the soldiers and other white men wore. These were very strange and both of them had something on the inside seam. It looked like centipedes were crawling up over his ankles, but the insects weren't moving. She'd keep an eye on them, just in case. Centipede bites hurt real bad and almost killed her best friend last year. She sighed in recall. Running Deer had survived the high fever, redness and swelling from the insect bite, but couldn't survive the high fever and red spots from the white man's disease, measles. She sure missed her—her and everyone else who had died.

Marty looked up from his fuel finding foray and saw stars. That was good news and bad news. The good news was it probably wouldn't rain tonight. The bad news is it would be getting cold, very cold. He looked around and saw Big Sister had spread out a deer hide on the ground and was rolling out her blanket on top of it. He watched as she set up another bed next to it. Probably for her father, he surmised. Then he realized what was so strange: except for the little hovel of a tent slash lean-to that the old women were housed in, there were no structures in this village. Then he remembered: measles. Whenever the measles struck an Indian village, the surviving members torched the homes and settled into a new site, leaving anything that had touched the 'bad medicine' burned to the ground along with their abodes. "Smart," he said softly, "gets rid of the germs even if it is a bit extreme."

Big Sister heard him speak in the strange tongue of the white man. Her uncle knew many words and had taught her a few of them—'hello,' 'please,' and 'thank you'—and had promised to

97

teach her a few more. He told her she would get more respect from the white man if she knew some of their language. If she didn't know any words, they would take advantage of her. But, he wouldn't teach her very many words. It was best for her to know just a few, he said, and let him deal with the white man.

Red Shirt walked up to Marty with a bundle under his arm. He looked Marty in the eye and returned his blanket roll to him, no words crossing his lips but his demeanor saying, 'Here, I think this is yours.'

"Why, thank you," Marty said politely. He was just deciding on whether to ask Red Shirt where he should bunk, or should he wait to be shown his spot, when the apparent chief dipped his head in farewell, a smirk growing on his face as he turned away to his own designated area. He was going to sleep with his wife again tonight. Marty watched as the hint of a smile blossomed into a full-blown grin of lust. No, he wouldn't break his friend's concentration; he'd just find his own empty space to drop his blanket then throw himself down on top of it. All of the sudden, the hard earth and lying horizontal sounded obscenely enticing. He had walked and trotted beside the horses all day. He was sixty-seven, no, sixty-eight years old. "I'm getting too old for this shit," he groaned as he picked up another armload of tree pieces to add to the woodpile.

Big Sister scurried over to his side and waited patiently for him to acknowledge her presence. "Please," the young girl said, and then pointed to an area on the opposite side of the fire from her. She had swept away the dropped twigs and kicked the larger stones from the new bedroom site for her tribe's guest, the man who was of use to them, the man who didn't know how to dress, the man her uncle called Dances Naked.

"Why, thank you very much," Marty replied and gave the lass a quick bow. "I appreciate the hospitality, miss. If there's anything I can assist you with, please don't hesitate to ask."

Big Sister's eyes widened on hearing so many words come out at one time. He talked more than Old Woman did! She didn't know what to do or say so nodded and said, "Thank you." She had already said 'please' and they were already in each other's presence so 'hello' wouldn't be appropriate so 'thank you' must be the right words.

Marty saw her shock then realized that he was being a bit too garrulous, again. Oh well, that's who he was and if he tried to be someone else, he'd risk Red Shirt not liking his fake persona. "Nope, 'to thine own self be true,' Melbourne. Now go to sleep."

Ж

Marty was awakened by a familiar foot prod. "Yesss," he drawled as he rolled over to see a stern-faced Red Shirt. He smiled at his new friend—he knew the near scowl was pasted on. He had heard the moans and giggles during the night and they weren't all from Red Shirt. Rachel seemed to like being a newlywed as much as her husband did.

Marty rolled up his blanket then looked around to find the best area to make his toilet. He saw Number Two coming back from what he hoped was the designated area, and then headed to the same cluster of bushes. When he came back, he saw that breakfast was going to consist of hot water. Hopefully, a town or trading post or whatever it was called, was nearby. He wasn't privy to the level of foodstores that this little tribe had but he was pretty sure that they were meager.

Red Shirt wasn't demonstrative but did take the time to pick up Junior again and hold him, tickling the boy's nose with the end of his finger. He waited for the lad to grab for it then pulled it away quickly. Smart father: teaching the boy to be swift at such a young age. Marty saw the tender look Rachel gave Red Shirt when she took her son back. She really was smitten with him and not just grateful to be out of a bad situation with her brother. Yes, Marty would be happy to help the extended family unit get back on their feet with the purchase of supplies, whether he got anything out of it or not. But, he still wanted to go home.

Red Shirt handed Marty the reins to the mare he once owned, motioning to him that he was to saddle up the horse.

"Sure," Marty replied. Yes, it would be wise of him to be on a saddled horse when he got to the store. He was already suspect; wearing a breechclout instead of pants, but a white man riding in on a blanket might look a bit strange. "Hmph," Marty grunted aloud. He was going to look odd no matter what. But then again, white men who traded with the Indians often took on their customs. "Hey," Marty called to Red Shirt, "If you don't want the saddle," he said as he pointed to it, now cinched up on the horse, "maybe I can trade for more food and supplies. Sound like a plan?"

Red Shirt knew what Dances Naked was saying and nodded in agreement. Yes, that was a good idea. He had thought of it, too, but hadn't wanted to suggest it to the white man. He'd save his words for another time. Besides, the two of them seemed to get along great when he didn't speak. "Hmph," he added, imitating the man's grunt: let's get going.

So, Red Shirt and Marty rode toward town, leaving The Young One and Number Two back at the camp. Marty didn't know if they were there for the clan's protection or if they were going hunting on their own. He hadn't heard of any military conflicts in the area but, then again, he hadn't been concerned with the war. All he had cared about was making sure that James made it to the right time and place and could save the life of his ancestor, Ian Kincaid. *And,* that he was there to meet him. He had missed James terribly and felt guilty about letting him believe that he had died alone, out at sea, of a mysterious terminal disease.

At least that was all he had cared about for the last six months. That mission had now been accomplished. Five days ago, the group had parted ways with new agendas. Wee Ian was left in charge of his wounded father. James and Leah's mission was to find the Pomeroy's Place and her mother. His mission, now, was to find his way back to The Trees, the time portal, so he could return to the 21st century; to Bibb, the love of his life, and Billy Burke, the son he never knew he had who for some strange reason had the same name as the actress who played Glinda, the Good Witch in The Wizard of Oz.

He was sure James and Leah had found their way to her mother. They had brought the necessary medical supplies and skills with them so Ian Kincaid would survive to sire Bibb's ancestors all the way down to James: his and Bibb's child. Children, sons, he had two sons alive now and the urgency to get back to the child, no, he was now a young man, whom he had never met, was starting to choke him, to cut off his air supply. "Ergh!" he grunted in frustration, and then realized that it was an audible exclamation—he hadn't just been thinking it.

"Sorry," he said to Red Shirt who was looking at him to see why he was making noises. Red Shirt gave him the 'whatever' look then kicked his pony in the flanks, picking up their pace. He wanted to get back to his family, too.

After a couple of hours of the quickened pace and one rest stop for another clear, aqueous meal: cold water, Red Shirt put his hand up for them to stop. He dismounted but indicated to Dances Naked that he should stay in the saddle. He pointed with his whole hand, shooing the air in front of him with the back of his fingers to indicate, 'Get going.'

Marty patted the lining of his vest then looked back at his friend. "I'll be quick about it then," he said in farewell.

He was just a few hundred yards from where the two of them had stopped when he saw the first signs of people: smoke from a fire. He wanted to race the nag to civilization, or at least to white people who would speak English, but trotted the horse to save her stamina. He wanted her to look good when he got there. He didn't want to present himself as a desperate man. People from all time eras had a tendency to take advantage of those in need or with only a few coins. He may not have pants but, hopefully, his bearing would override that little shortcoming.

"Hey, there," Marty called out to the man walking outside toward the little outbuilding behind the long, log house.

"Hey," the man replied in a congenial manner, "Be right with ye. I have a bit of important business to take care of first."

Marty realized that his first impression was correct. That tidy little shed really was an outhouse. "A wooden seated privy," he sighed. "Lord, what I wouldn't do for inside plumbing…oops, sorry, Lord," he said softly. "It's just the hunger talking. Please guide me in this transaction to get food for these people and keep Bibb and Billy and James and Leah safe. And, sorry I haven't been talking to you lately. Oh, here he comes, Amen."

"So, are ye a priest or a preacher?" the amiable man asked as he exited the privy. "I heard ye talkin' to the Lord so I figured ye must be one of them."

"No, no," Marty admitted, "I just know He's the man in charge and I was asking Him for some help in my shopping here today. I need as many food supplies as I can get with these few coins," he added as he traced the slight bulge in the lining of his vest. "I have quite a few in my family and we're just about all out of food."

"Well, come on in and let's see what we have. I'm Michael, by the way. Ye dinna happen to have any furs to trade, do ye? I could do better with furs than with the coin. I have a buyer for the furs but, with this confounded war going on, not many trappers are workin' the rivers and streams. They're too busy shootin' at each other!" The tall, wiry, silver-haired storekeeper brushed some yellow grit from the front of his apron. "But if yer needin' cornmeal, I can probably do ye a good deal on that. It seems like everyone that's come in lately has that to trade. Come to think about it, yer coin might be useful in another matter. The tinker's due through here before the snow falls. He likes the coin and I'm pretty sure he's had his fair share of cornmeal, too," he said then laughed heartily.

Marty stooped over and retrieved his boot knife then brought it up to his vest. He cut a few stitches and six coins fell out of their discreet binding. "How much will this get me?" Marty asked. "And remember, I have a big family."

"I can do, hmm, let's say four of the big bags of cornmeal, and do ye need any flour?" he asked.

"Some flour and a ham if you have one, or even bacon—yes, definitely bacon. I don't need any coffee or sugar but I'm totally out of salt," Marty babbled. He was getting light-headed from lack of food. "And can I have some of those candies? I'd like a peppermint right now if you don't mind. My stomach's, um, a little upset." Marty realized he wasn't lying—his stomach was upset, with him, for not putting any food in it all day.

"Here ye go," Michael said as he handed him a round, striped candy. "But I'm sorry. Fer jest these few coins, I canna be lettin' ye have the meat. Ye can have the cornmeal and a bag of the flour and a bit of salt, but no meat. No charge fer the candy I jest gave ye, but no more."

Marty set his knife on the counter then opened out the other side of his vest. He picked up the knife again, made another slit, and extracted six more coins. "Ham and bacon?" he asked as he pushed the coins toward Michael, "and a few candies?" he added with a pepperminty smile.

"Yer a sly one, ye are," Michael chortled. "Aye, a couple, no, I'll make that three rashers of bacon and a bag of the candies, but I only have the one ham and I was savin' it fer a wedding. That is if my daughter ever gets married!" he said with a mixture of mirth and frustration.

"You're sure that's the best you can do for the twelve coins: cornmeal, flour, salt, bacon and a few candies? How about cabbages or potatoes? I could carry those and they'd sure make a fine stew, if I had some meat," Marty hinted. "Or oats, surely a fine man like you, Scottish, aye, would have a nice, big bag of rolled oats to offer to feed my starvin' family."

"How many did ye say were in yer family?" Michael asked before committing to adding any more supplies for the twelve coins. He enjoyed the bartering and didn't mind making a healthy profit, but this man did look needy and a bit of alms given to a poor family would make him look good in the eyes of the Lord.

"Well, we had some sickness and death just recently and a birth so," Marty drew out the drama and started counting on his fingers, adding with a smile the new child, Junior; then frowned at a loss, Number Two's wife. "Including me and the in-laws and old grandma, there's thirteen. We're down to our last bag of cornmeal and that'll probably be gone by the time I get back. We've been having naught but water for some meals," Marty said sincerely, his stomach grumbling in agreement with his dissertation.

"Weel, I guess I can throw in a bag of the tatties and I have a few more cabbages than we need. Do ye think ye could use a few onions? I had a great harvest of those and I'd rather give them away than have them sit around and spoil, waitin' fer spring."

"Well, that's mighty generous of you, Michael. We would all appreciate it. As a matter of fact, I may just give the next child born your name. I mean, without your generosity, we might not make it 'to' winter much less 'through' winter."

Michael tried to hide the smile of pride that he felt: someone was going to name a child after him for giving him his extra food, but couldn't contain his excitement and went ahead and let loose his grin. "Weel, I jest hope it's a boy. With a name like Michael, a lass might get teased a bit," he said joyfully as he gathered the empty, used calico flour bags from the corner. "I'll be right back with the vegetables; they're in the cold cellar."

Marty waited until the spirited storekeeper was out of sight then said a quick prayer. "Thank you, Lord, for the bounty. And may he be as blessed by You as he has been a blessing to us."

104

Michael stopped short as he heard the words. He was going to load the rotted cabbages and potatoes on the bottom of the bags; he didn't want to throw those into the compost pit if he could make a profit on them, but changed his mind. The blessing he had just received could be turned into a curse for doing a bad deed. "Sorry, Lord, fer the bad intent," he said under his breath then filled the bags with the prime fruits of the autumn's harvest. He left the bags on the porch and came back inside. "I'll jest sew these bags up so they don't spill and ye can be on yer way to yer family. I'm sure they'll be happy to see ye."

"Me and the food!" Marty proclaimed then laughed. He brought his emotions down a couple of levels and got serious. "I have a fine saddle out there and, um, I know you said that you were saving the ham for your daughter's wedding, if she has one this year, but do you think that you'd consider trading the ham for my saddle? I mean, you and I know that it's worth a lot more, but I really would like to bring home some meat. The hunting hasn't been very, oh well, I haven't shot a deer in so long, I don't know if I'd know what to do with one," Marty said in exasperation. It was the truth and he knew it showed. He didn't want or need the saddle but did want to insure that, even if they didn't get any game in the next few months, his new little tribe wouldn't starve to death.

Michael walked out and inspected the saddle. The horse wasn't the greatest but the saddle was quite nice. "The saddlebags, too?" Michael asked warily. He knew it was a great deal even without them.

Marty sighed deeply. He was probably being taken advantage of—no, he definitely was—but he wanted to get the deal done and get the ham and other food back to Red Shirt then to the others. "If you truly, honestly believe that it's a good trade, my saddle and saddlebags for one ham, then I'll do it. But just remember, in the words of my father and his father before him, 'What goes around, comes around.'" Marty saw the confused look on the trader's face so explained further. "How you treat me is how you will be treated in the future, aye?"

Michael's neck pulled back in shock. He never thought of it that way. "Oh, of course I'll give you some beans to go with the ham. I mean, that's the second best part of the ham, having ham and beans for the next six meals!"

Marty pulled the saddle and saddlebags off the mare and repositioned the saddle blanket while Michael went to his cold cellar to retrieve not one but two hams. They weren't the biggest ones he had, they were actually quite modest, but there were two of them. As Marty arranged his bounty on the back of the mare, now his packhorse, Michael brought out two more bags. "I forgot about the oats. The wee'uns need to have their porritch. And dinna forget about namin' the next child Michael, now, hear?" the wiry man said with a grin.

"And if it's a lass, we can always call her Michelle," Marty said as he stuck out his hand for a proper handshake to seal to the deal. He threw the bag of oats over one shoulder and the beans over the other. The horse was loaded with enough food to feed Red Shirt's little tribe for months. It was a good day.

12 Dear Prudence

Marty looked like a colorful two-legged camel as he portaged the two bulging, reclaimed calico flour sacks: rolled oats over one shoulder and beans over the other. He strode joyfully ahead of the grocery-laden horse; chin out with pride. He beamed as he realized that he was doing more than fine—he was alive, alert, able to walk, and had a destination. The mare was well watered and so was he. He had taken the opportunity to drink right alongside his equine lady friend before they left. She had taken advantage of a free meal, nibbling the tough grass that had sprouted up next to the trough, while he was inside bartering. His stomach rumbled at the thought of food. At least the mare's stomach could handle the ancient, golden sprouts. He wasn't that desperate—yet. He'd bide and wait to get back to camp to eat with the others.

Marty turned and waved good-bye one more time to Michael then headed into the dense scrub. He breathed a sigh of relief. His hopes had been fulfilled: he had food for his friends. Family. Both. He shook his head gently in dismay—his thoughts weren't coming together like they should. Instead of progressing in a straight line, they were flitting around like drunken butterflies. It was nothing to worry about though. He knew the cause: he was lightheaded from the lack of food.

"Oh, well," he commented as he realized that, no matter what, the future was bright. He knew he'd be back to his normal, clearheaded self after consuming a few of the calories that he was toting on his and the mare's backs. He grabbed her reins and trotted ahead of her, setting a comfortable pace for the two of them. There was too much loaded on her back for him to ride and that was just fine with him. He'd rather jog alongside a food-laden, bareback horse than ride a saddled one with empty bags and belly. Yes, it was a good day and he had done well with his bartering. Red Shirt would be proud of him.

Red Shirt saw Dances Naked running in front of his mare, their two heads bouncing just above the short trees and tall bushes that led away from the white man's store. 'Well, at least he didn't lose my horse,' he thought. He couldn't see if the crazy white man had been successful in spending his coins, but at least he hadn't been robbed, and could still walk. No, he was almost running. Yes, he was still healthy enough to run and wise enough to return to him. He never threatened Dances Naked; he didn't feel like he had to, but he would have hunted him down and eaten his liver if he had tried to take his horse and leave rather than trade his coins for food like he had offered. Red Shirt nodded. Yes, he was still a good judge of character.

Red Shirt rode his stallion to the spot where he would intercept the running white man. He snorted. The funny man would probably get lost trying to find his way back to the camp if he didn't have a guide—he was already veering away from where he should be. Dances Naked had no sense of direction and, from what he could gather, wasn't from this area. He got lost very easily, even for a white man.

"Hey, there!" Marty called out when he spotted Red Shirt. "I hit the jackpot!" he said breathlessly, quickening his pace to reach the man sooner. He knew as soon as the words were out of his mouth, Red Shirt couldn't possibly know what he was talking about He'd wait until he caught his wind and was closer to explain though. Then again, when his friend saw all the booty, no explanation would be necessary.

Red Shirt's eyes widened in shock—both the horse and the white man were loaded with colorful bags of provisions. His mouth spread wide into an uninhibited smile, his lips parting to show both his teeth and his happiness. There was enough food for his family for months.

"You like?" Marty asked, grinning just as much his friend.

"I like," Red Shirt replied then slipped off his horse. He reached for the two bags of food Marty was carrying then threw them over his own shoulders. He nodded to Marty: you ride.

"Me?" Marty asked although he knew without a doubt, that was what he meant.

Red Shirt grunted: 'Don't make me offer again.'

"Okay, okay, thank you," Marty babbled then put his hand on the stallion's mane and made a valiant attempt at mounting him. "Um, he's a bit taller than most and I'm used to stirrups and my legs are a bit wobbly…" Marty carped, half seriously, half in jest and totally embarrassed.

Red Shirt sighed and stood next to him, squatted down a little and cupped his hands to give Marty a boost. As it was, it still took two attempts to get the worn out and undernourished old man onto the now skittish stallion's back. "I got it, I got it," Marty announced when settled with the leather reins in his hands. "You lead and I'll follow," he said as he looked to his friend and nodded to where he thought they were going.

The chief set a double time pace which was easy for the horse and easier still for Marty but had to be taking its toll on the proud red man. After about an hour, Marty noticed his pace slowing. "Eh, hmm; eh, hmm," Marty vocalized loudly to get Red Shirt's attention. It worked. Both of them stopped and Marty started right in with his excuse. "I need to, um, make water, so can we take just a moment here?" he said, and then slid off the horse without waiting for an answer. He made sure he held onto the reins then turned his back and relieved himself. He took an extra minute; presumably, to make sure all was taken care of, but actually allowing a bit more recovery time for the two-legged porter of the provisions. When he turned back around, he saw that Red Shirt had set down his bags and was taking a long drink of water from the canteen. He finished his refreshment then offered it to Marty.

Marty accepted it, took a couple of gulps, and then handed it back. "I got a little something to take care of the sour stomach," he said then loosed a few stitches in the bag of beans and retrieved the little paper wrapped parcel of peppermint candies. He knew nothing had been said or inferred about bellyaches, but the candy he had eaten at the store had quelled his fire—maybe his friend was suffering from the same malady. And, a little sugar coated calorie cube might help make the last leg of the journey a little easier, too. He would have offered to swap places with Red Shirt but figured that would probably be an insult to his proud companion.

Red Shirt took the white and red rock-shaped piece he was offered. He knew Dances Naked wouldn't present him with bad food or insult him in any way. The food he had shared with him when they first met, a strange nut, was good. He'd try this, too.

Marty saw the look on Red Shirt's face, suggesting that he take one, too. "No thanks; I already had one. It's a peppermint. Don't bite it," he mimed crunching down on the candy then shook his head, "just suck on it." Marty puckered his lips and swished his cheeks around, making an exaggerated gesture to elicit a slight grin from his traveling buddy. Red Shirt sniffed the candy then ventured a quick lick to prepare his mouth. The nut was salty—would this be, too? Nope—this tasted like the green plant that grew under the trees near water. Yes, it was good for a sour belly, but this food was sweet, too. He plopped the whole piece in his mouth, involuntarily smiling at the sweetness, and then nodded to Marty: get on the horse.

Marty had stopped at this site on purpose. There were boulders littering the landscape and one was sure to be just the right height to use as an equine mounting apparatus. He walked the steed to a likely platform, climbed the rock, and brought the horse closer to him. He had to take a little leap but still made it astride the steed without Red Shirt having to act as his footman. Next stop: his new, albeit temporary, home.

Ж

This time Red Shirt was confident, not leery, as he approached the almost-a-village site. He was returning as a victor, not empty handed and with three more mouths to feed. This should shut up Old Woman.

The matriarch exited her little twig and hide castle of prominence to see what her grandson had brought to share. He had embarrassed her last time. Hopefully, he wouldn't do it again. He was her son's son, tall and intelligent, but too meek and forgiving to be a real man. And, he was not a very good hunter, either. Their tribe would perish under him if she didn't intercede. He had convinced his father that he should learn the white man's tongue. The months he was away, learning the white men's ways, were the ones when he was needed the most, when the red belly sickness came. It would have been better if he had died of the measles and his father had lived. Yes, if his father had lived, maybe he could have sired another son, one who was a strong warrior, who listened to his gut and not his heart like her grandson whom she secretly called, 'My Shame.'

Marty stopped the horse with a stern, "whoa," and a tug on the reins as soon as he saw they were just outside of their little village. He slipped down and ran to catch up with Red Shirt who had evidently gotten a second or third wind with the excitement of coming home. "Here," he said as he put the reins in the hand of the man-who-was-probably-chief's hand. "Let me take the bags. You're the boss and I'm just the facilitator, I mean," he stammered trying to figure a way to say in simple words that they needed to be politically correct in their presentation. He retrieved the bag of oats from a perplexed Red Shirt and put his shoulder under it. "You're the chief, I'm not," he said simply, then turned his unburdened shoulder to his friend, asking him without words to 'load me up' with the bag of beans. He'd come into town as a slave, or worker at least, not riding on the man-in-charge's stallion.

Red Shirt gave a quick chuckle of chagrin and nodded to Dances Naked. He was slightly embarrassed that in his exhilaration to be home with food, lots of food, he had forgotten his position. He already owed this white friend a favor for the food, maybe a trip to The Terrible Trees— but then again, maybe not. However, now he had also spared him shame in front of his family and most important of all, his grandmother. He nodded once more to Dances Naked and grinned. 'Yes, you got yourself a guide to your Trees—I owe you that,' he said without words.

It was nice that this man could understand him. He had already used three of the white man's words with him. His father had told him that when he had used ten of their words to any one man, it was time for him to go. Hopefully, no, he was sure, that did not pertain to a woman. He had already used more than ten words with his wife and that was in only two days. He was going to keep her no matter how many words he said to her, but he'd say them in private. She'd learn his tongue faster if he could teach her with shared words. He'd let her speak the English to their son when no one else could hear. That would help him when he grew to be a man, just as it had helped him many times in the last year. But, he couldn't tell anyone about those times. They were secret and not to be shared with anyone.

The six-legged grocery store strode through the micro village, both men, and even the horses, holding their heads high in pride. Red Shirt knew it would be proper to acknowledge Old Woman first, but she had tried to humiliate him in front of his tribe. There were only ten of them left, no, twelve with his new wife and son, but he still should be respected and not ignored. He would have counted Dances Naked as the thirteenth member but he wouldn't be staying. He would like to have him remain—he was dependable, clever, and made him smile—but he knew the man needed to be back with his woman and child. Yes, he'd take the food to the loyal members of his tribe first.

The men and the horses passed in front the old crones' hut without stopping, heading straight to the heart and core of his tribe.

Then he saw it.

Red Shirt's golden glow of pride exploded into a red rage of anger striped with green lightning bolts of jealousy: Number Two was sitting next to his wife, looking at her and, it appeared to be, touching her as only a husband should touch a wife.

Red Shirt dismounted and hit the ground running, ready to tackle his brother-in-law for improper advances toward his wife. "Whoa, whoa, whoa!" yelled Marty as he quickly pulled in his shoulders to drop his dry goods, unabashedly chasing after his new best friend to stop him before he did something rash. "It's not what it looks like, I'm sure it's not!"

Marty literally stood between the two men, his arms held out straight to separate them, one hand on each man's shoulder. "Rachel, button up," he commanded. "You," he glared at Red Shirt, "wait to do or say anything until we find out what's going on here. And you," he ordered Number Two, "take your son and daughter and sit down over there," Marty nodded to a neutral corner. He knew there would be less chance of fisticuffs, or anything else, if the man was holding a baby and had his daughter at his elbow.

"Rachel, did Number Two touch you inappropriately or," Marty saw the confused look on her face and spoke as if to a six-year-old, "Did he touch you in a way that made you feel bad."

"No, he touched his son's head when I was nursing him. He mumbled some words but I don't know what he was saying. But, he didn't touch me at all. I think he was just saying, 'Thank you.' At least I think that's what he was trying to say." Rachel finished her explanation with a sad, scared, and repentant look to

Red Shirt that said, 'Nothing was going on, I promise. I'm sorry if you got the wrong impression.'

Marty looked to Number Two. "You don't, um, want her," he asked, then gave a crude gesture with his right index finger entering his left, curled fist, indicating sexual intercourse, "that way, do you?"

Number Two's head pulled back in shock, shaking it rapidly, his body language screaming, 'No! That's my brother-in-law's wife! What, do you think I'm crazy?'

Marty looked at Red Shirt to see if he saw the reaction. "Hmph," was his monosyllabic response. 'Yes, I see now; just don't ever do it again.'

"I think he was thanking you for the milk. I don't think he'll get that close to say 'thanks' again," Marty said with a sigh then added a stern look to Number Two.

Big Sister stood up and ran to Rachel, squatted next to her, and touched her hand to the blouse covering her new aunt's breast. "Thank you," she said clearly, then ran back to her father and baby brother. She'd speak for her father if he couldn't, or wouldn't, use the white man's words. Sometimes men were so stubborn.

"So we're all cool here? I mean, it's good, right?" Marty said, nodding his head to each one in the little discussion circle. Each person nodded in agreement so Marty changed the subject, ready to get back to the main program. He tipped his head to Red Shirt in introduction, "Everyone here ready to eat? Red Shirt here managed to get us a *lot* of food. He's a great provider."

Red Shirt grabbed the reins of his mare and walked her forward, patting the bags of food on her back then pointing to the two calico bags on the ground that Marty had dropped, totally ignoring the near fatal collision caused by his jealous rage at the apparent Lothario. He turned his back on the familial gathering, untied the cord, and turned back to present to them the best of the best: a ham.

Marty peered around Red Shirt and his horse. He could see that his friend knew what was going on behind him—he wasn't deaf. The thunk, thunk of the wooden staff was unmistakable: Old Woman had come to him and his outcasts for food. She glared at her grandson—he hadn't stopped to pay his respects to her before coming to his other family.

Red Shirt took it in stride. She wouldn't embarrass him ever again. Her vicious words still hurt even if they were many months old. She blamed him for the death of his father, wife, son, and everyone else, telling the others that he was the one who brought the red belly sickness to them. She knew it wasn't true: he had already been gone for one month when the first one died. How could he have brought the disease if he hadn't yet returned? Only the other old women believed her. He'd let them eat, too, but he'd feed his faithful family first.

Red Shirt carved into the widest portion of the ham, extracting a half-inch steak, then held it up for everyone to see. He raised the meat to the sky and proclaimed bold, strong words in his language. "Thanks, Lord," Marty offered softly at the same time, loud enough to show God he wasn't embarrassed to praise Him, but low enough to be respectful of Red Shirt and his words of thanksgiving to his Great Spirit. They were the same, he surmised, but he wasn't the chief, Red Shirt was, and this was his ceremony.

Red Shirt cut the filet into small strips, handing one to each member of his tribe, the first one going to Number Two, the man who he was ready to kill just moments earlier. All was forgiven—you are still my second in command. The Young One got the next slice and then, Marty was shocked, he got the third piece. He noticed each one held on to his share of the sacrament, waiting for the chief to serve everyone. Red Shirt gave Rachel her portion next, then Big Sister, and on down the line until last, and apparently least, Old Woman got hers.

Each person raised his share to the sky and joined in the 'blah, blah' to say thank you for the bounty. Red Shirt bit into his strip of ham and chewed slowly, his glow of satisfaction unmistakable. He wouldn't have any more problems with his grandmother and the other old women. If anyone died this winter, it wouldn't be his fault.

Red Shirt took the honor of unloading the bounty, passing the bags to his braves who ferried them to the empty dugout cache. The stone and timber shelter carved into the side of a hillock was for smoking meat but would be fine for keeping the food cool and safe from predators. Marty neared the trio pensively, not knowing if he would be out of line if he volunteered to help. 'Hmph, they never seemed to resent me before,' he said to himself. "Need a hand there?" he asked the men without reservation.

Red Shirt patted the coarse burlap bag, trying to figure out what the lumps were. They weren't heavy enough to be rocks and didn't feel hard like a gourd. He looked at Marty, 'What are these?' he asked with his scowl.

"Oh, these are potatoes," Marty explained as he took the coarse sack from him. He paused at the campfire before taking the spuds to the food locker. "You know how to fix these, don't you?" he asked Rachel who had been watching the proceedings with a baby on each knee, not quite sure what she was supposed to be doing to help.

Rachel nodded and said, "I put them in stew," then added in a whisper as he set the bag down next to her, "but I didn't see any pots around here, just earthen bowls. I don't know if they have any."

"Well," Marty said assertively, "then we'll just have to have baked potatoes. We don't need anything but fire for that, and since you already have one going, let's just rub the dirt off of these, hmm…" He was telling her to rub off the dirt then stuff them under embers and more dirt. "Oh well, just scrub them up a bit, poke them a few times with a sharp stick then bury them under the coals for an hour or so. Pull one of them out when you start to smell them and see if it's soft. If they are, just pop 'em open with a knife and toss a bit of salt on them and *manga!* I mean, and then eat them when they've cooled off enough so as not to burn your fingers or tongue. They'd be even better with a big dollop of butter, but salt will be just fine for now."

Rachel pulled eleven of the fair-sized spuds out of the bag and began rubbing off the caked mud. Big Sister saw what the task entailed and hurried over to her new aunt's side, eager to be of assistance in preparing food. She'd never eaten anything like this but was willing to try. She had only eaten dried fish and cornmeal for months. The smoked meat, ham Rachel called it, was good, but made her thirsty. That was okay. Water would take care of that. At least she was drinking water for thirst, not to fill her belly.

Marty looked around and noticed that something was different. The old women had decided that they would stay and make sure they got more food beyond the sliver of ham. Either that or they were too weak to return to their little hovel. Nah, they wanted the food. Old Woman was still at it, clamoring away in her choppy tongue, by the rhythm of the chatter, complaining about something. Marty looked over at the three braves. Yup, by the glower on all three of their faces, she was carping about how long it was taking for the meal to be readied. Well, she'd just have to wait like everyone else.

After about an hour, Marty noticed the men's noses wrinkling up, and then he noticed it, too: the potatoes were done. Rachel was right on top of it and used a stick to pull out one of the spuds, using her skirt as a makeshift plate. "Let it cool a couple of minutes," he advised. "It's still cooking on the inside and will give you a steam burn if you cut it open too soon." He walked over to her impromptu dinner table and lightly tapped the potato. It was soft enough but not too mushy. "Go ahead and pull the others out—they should be done, too."

Rachel lifted her skirt to keep the first of the spuds contained then neared the fire and used her stick to pull out the others. "Just set them out on the ground next to each other. We don't want you catching your skirt on fire," Marty said. He was pretty sure that wouldn't happen, but didn't want her to be chance it. She'd have to start wearing clothing more appropriate to her new status as wife of the chief.

After ten minutes, Marty remembered the seasoning. "Did you happen to keep out some salt?" he asked. Rachel seemed to have become the woman in charge, even if she was white. By the look of relief on Big Sister's face, she was glad to have someone else take over the role.

"I got a bowl of it right here," Rachel replied as she held up a brown earthen bowl. "Um, how much longer do we have to wait?"

Red Shirt looked to Marty for the answer, too. Marty touched the top of a potato and left his finger there for a moment then pulled it back: it wasn't too hot. He picked it up and tossed it from one hand to the other, smiling as he remembered playing 'hot potato' with James when he was about Big Sister's age. He started to toss it to her then remembered his place in this society. Handing out the food was Red Shirt's responsibility and right. He replaced the spud and stepped back. "They're ready, sir," he said reverently to Red Shirt then bowed to him respectfully.

Red Shirt picked up all of the potatoes and cradled them in his arms. Marty's eyes popped wide: they were still plenty hot. He was probably getting second-degree burns on his arms from the load, but there wasn't a show of pain in Red Shirt's face, only pride.

Yes, these tubers were hot, hotter than he had expected, but he would not drop them or rush in giving one to each member of his tribe. The faithful would be served first and receive the largest ones, the fussy old women would have to wait for theirs. Suddenly, the food wasn't so hot anymore. He'd move just a little slower so they had to wait longer. But, he would still feed them. Maybe next time they'd listen to him, not 'her.'

Marty took out his little boot knife and cut into the potato, pushing in on the ends and sides to open up the steaming pulp inside. He saw that he was the demonstrator on how to eat this new food. Even Rachel wasn't used to eating baked potatoes. "Salt, please," he asked her. Whether or not he was being correct in the Cherokee mealtime etiquette, they were still looking to him for instruction.

Rachel passed the salt then reached for the knife used for cooking, copying Marty's slash, slash, push, push technique to prep the potato. He passed the salt back to her then decided he'd use the knife as a fork...at least until he got to the end when he'd chew the insides like watermelon off a rind, saving the best until last, the skin. Marty looked around and saw that everyone was copying him. Apparently, even the old women had knives and were employing them, deftly cutting into then sniffing the white, fluffy insides. They weren't too sure about the new food, but the white man seemed to enjoy it. At least it shouldn't make them sick if he was eating it, too.

"Hey, this is good," commented Rachel with mouth full as she fed a bit to Junior. "They're easy to fix, too." She swallowed and asked sincerely, "Do these grow on trees?"

Marty choked back a laugh, pretending that it was from food that had gone down the wrong pipe, patting his chest in both physical and emotional recovery. "No, no, these grow underground. That's why there was dirt on them." Marty saw Rachel cringe in embarrassment. He hadn't intended to make her feel ignorant. "But they do look like they'd grow on a tree and just fall onto the ground when they were ripe...that's why they'd be dirty." Rachel gave a weak smile. She knew he was covering up for embarrassing her.

"Now, I don't know how long I'm going to be here. I think your husband," Marty said and watched her glow with the designation, "will be taking me, um, home, in a few days or weeks or, ahem." He cleared his throat that was starting to tighten with hope at the mention of being back with Bibb and tried again, "What I'm trying to say is that I won't be here in the spring. I want you to make sure you hold back a dozen or so, at least, of the potatoes to plant when the ground warms up but before the rains. Those little dimples that were in the spuds, potatoes, are called eyes." Rachel pulled her head back and Marty saw that Red Shirt was listening to him, too, and was also shocked at the word.

"They're called eyes but what they really are, are places where the sprouts start for a new plant. By springtime, you'll see what I mean. What you need to do is cut each potato into segments so that each one has about three," he held up three fingers and wiggled them, "sprouts. Let the potato cuts dry out for a few days and then plant each chunk, that is, piece, in a trench, about two feet apart. Only put about so much," he spread his fingers about an inch apart, "dirt on top. The little sprouts will start to turn into leaves. Keep burying the new plants with a bit more dirt every week or two until you have a hill. New little potatoes will form underground. If you get hungry and can't wait until harvest, that's after the plant has bloomed and then withered, you can burrow into the hills and pull out what they call new potatoes. They don't have the tough skin on them and you can't save them as long as the mature ones, but they taste even better, at least to me they do. So, do you think you can be the chief cook, bottle washer, and farmer?" he asked with a smile.

"Bottle washer?" Rachel asked. She already knew what cooks and farmers were.

"Oh, just, I mean, the one to take care of feeding the babies," he fumbled. She wouldn't understand the innuendo about breastfeeding, bottle-feeding and washing bottles anyhow.

"Yes, I can take care of the babies, and Big Sister helps with the cooking, and I'm sure she'll help with the farming, too. But I don't think they have any bottles around here so that's a good thing, I think," she said, still confused.

Suddenly everyone's attention was at the far end of the camp. Old Woman had been tottering back to her makeshift palace with her cronies when something startled her. "Blah, blah, blah!" she shouted then repeated her threat again, verbatim, "Blah, blah, blah!"

The three braves rushed to her aid. Big Sister pulled Rachel and the babies back to her, protecting them as only a six-year-old with an attitude could. 'Stay with me. I won't let anyone hurt you,' she said with her stance.

Then Marty heard it. Or rather, he heard her. "I don't mean you any harm. I was just looking for the white man who came to our store earlier," she said, a false bravado unsuccessfully trying to cover the squeak of fear as the word 'our' came out.

Marty hopped over the fire, skipped then ran over to the gathering, hoping to avert any problems before they started. Old Woman was shaking her staff at a white woman, trying to terrorize her with the end of it from a safe ten paces away. They were both scared—that he could see. Red Shirt was at the perimeter of the fracas. Marty couldn't see his face but he'd just about bet that he was smiling at the confrontation.

"Hi, you were looking for me?" he asked as he stepped into the low glow of the campfire. The old women had been at the dinner party and had let their fire burn low. He stooped down and threw a couple more faggots onto the embers. The light would hopefully brighten the attitude and douse the eerie feeling that the low light created.

"Yes, I thought that, um," she faltered then inhaled sharply. She had already made her decision and now she would have to stick with it. She started again, "I thought that you might need a pot for all those beans that you got…and maybe a bread pan or two," she added, suddenly feeling braver.

A young, fine-figured white woman with an oversized cap walked into the light, a lumpy green cotton print bag in one hand, a fancy, carpetbag satchel in the other. She pulled her shoulders back proudly then walked toward Marty, her head bowing sharply just before she got to him, hiding something.

"Why, I thank you for the gift, gifts," he corrected then leaned sideways to see why she was hiding her face. "Is there something wrong?" he asked. "I mean, surely you shouldn't be out here at night, all by yourself, should you?"

"No and yes. Or yes and no. Shoot," she exclaimed, suddenly frustrated and showing a true emotion for the first time. She took two small steps back away from him and began her heartfelt explanation. "I guess I'm running away from home. I overheard you tell my father that you had a big family and, and, well…I'm running away from home and would like to stay with you." Her confidence faded quickly as she added, "But I didn't think you had an Indian family. I mean, I only heard you, I didn't see you. I mean, I didn't know you didn't wear pants!" she said in exasperation.

"Well, I do sometimes," Marty admitted with a chuckle. "It's just I got such a good deal on a trade for this…" he joked as he flipped the edge of his breechclout. Marty looked around at the stern faces of the old women, Red Shirt and the other two braves. They weren't impressed with his casual banter with the female intruder. He had to do some quick damage control.

"I think you've put us at risk," he said somberly. "It's going to look like you've been kidnapped, at least. White women don't just walk up to Indians and say I want to be part of your family."

"Yes, they do," Rachel piped up, Junior on her hip, Big Sister on the other side, holding Baby Brother.

"Well, not very often," Marty corrected. "But you didn't have any family, not really," he added softly to Rachel, "and you do," he said sternly to the woman, her age still indeterminable. "Are you the one who your father was hoping would get married soon; that he was saving the big ham for your wedding?" he asked.

"Yes," she replied dejectedly. "But I didn't want to get married, to, ugh, the man he wanted me to marry. And anyone that I, um, liked, wouldn't look at me, at least look at me twice." The young woman set her bags down at her side and walked closer to Marty and the firelight, and then pulled back her wide flounced mobcap. "See," she said with a shrug of her shoulder.

Old Woman started in again, "Blah, blah, blah! Blah, blah, blah!"

Marty looked over at her and said coldly, "Shut up, Old Woman." He heard Red Shirt and Number Two snort quickly, an outburst of laughter sneaking past their lips then contained just as fast as it had slipped out. Marty looked back to the generous visitor and said, "Okay, so you've got a port wine stain birthmark on your cheek. So what? You seem intelligent, obviously have a kind heart or you wouldn't be sharing, must be healthy if you could walk all the way here…You did walk, didn't you? I mean, I'd hate to be accused of horse stealing, too."

"No, I walked," she said.

"But you've placed us in an awkward position. As I was saying, I'm sure your father will be out looking for you in the morning, if he isn't already. Say, how did you find us? I mean, I had a hard time finding this place and I'd been here before and had a guide."

"I, um, cut a hole in one of the bags of cornmeal. It wasn't a big hole, just enough so a few grains of meal slipped out." The woman saw Marty's stern scowl and added, "But I only saw the trail because I was looking for it. You must have stopped once because there was a bigger pile of it by some rocks, but I covered it up with dirt. Nobody will find me, us. I promise. Besides, I left a note for my father. I said I was going to Washington to catch a ship and sail to England. I have an uncle there and he said I could stay with him anytime." The girl huffed with confidence at her cleverness, just coming short of issuing an 'hmph!' in satisfaction.

"Washington? D.C.?" Marty asked. Surely, she couldn't mean Washington State—that was still wild country and on the northwest coast of America.

"No," she replied and shook her head, wondering what he was talking about. "They used to call it Forks of the Tar. They changed the name a few years ago in honor of General George Washington. Big ships come in and go out of there all the time. I was going to sell my pendant for passage to England." The young woman smiled broadly. "At least that's what I said in the letter. I know it's a sin to lie, but I told father that the tinker agreed to take me to Washington as a favor to him, not to worry about me, and that I would write to him when I got to England and Uncle Remus."

Marty looked to Red Shirt for the answer to the question on everyone's mind: what are we going to do with her? He was just the interrogator. If Red Shirt didn't understand everything she had said, he at least got the gist of her story. Letting her stay with them was a gamble. Either way, they couldn't send her back in the middle of the night. She'd have to stay at least until morning.

Red Shirt canted his head at Marty then looked to the pretty woman with the purple mark on her face. 'Bring her to our camp—she can stay the night,' he said with his body language.

"Well, it looks like you can stay here at least until morning. I'm Marty Melbourne, by the way. And you are?" he asked, waiting for her to answer.

"Prudence. Prudence Huntsman, but I'll take any name they want to give me," she said as she nodded to the apparent man in charge.

Marty watched the three braves watch the woman as she watched them. Number Two's eyes were smiling even if his mouth wasn't. His brother-in-law had just found a white wife—maybe he could have this one.

"Come on, Miss Waiting-for-a-new-name," Marty said as he moved toward her bags. Number Two rushed over and picked up her carpet bag before Marty could retrieve it then reached around her and grabbed the kitchen cookware duffel, too, wordlessly offering his services as porter. Marty tucked his chin in and dropped his jaw, surprised at the white glove service the problematic intruder was receiving. Maybe there was going to be a new Mrs. Number Two soon.

"Why, thank you," she said and smiled at the good-looking man who had just taken the bags for her. "You are such a gentleman."

'Maybe 'very' soon,' Marty thought silently. It could be that Rachel and Big Sister would have help with the cooking, farming, and bottle washing.

13 Morning Star

Number Two led the ladies to the campfire, dropped the bags without a word or even a grunt, then went into the shadows. He would watch this new white woman and see if she should stay or be returned to her family. It would be Red Shirt's decision but he would ask for her if he thought she would be a good wife and mother to his children.

Big Sister took Prudence's hand and pointed to the cleared area on the other side of her bedding. "Please," she said, offering her the warmest place available.

"Thank you," she replied then sat down, crossing her legs under her ample skirts, covertly surveying the isolated location. Yes, this place would not be easy to find without a guide, good directions, or a cornmeal trail. Even if her father suspected that she had followed Marty, he still wouldn't be able to locate this site.

Big Sister situated herself next to the lady with the big, strange hat, shifting her brother to her shoulder so she could sit closer to her. "She's beautiful," Prudence commented then frowned and lifted the tyke's long shirt. "He's very handsome," she said, correcting herself. "Where's your mother?" she asked cautiously as she accepted the boy into her arms, glowing at the trust the young girl was showing her by letting her hold the baby.

"She died, of the measles, I think," Rachel answered in resignation as she came to sit down in the empty spot in the little impromptu parlor. "I've only been with this tribe for two days. I'm Rachel, Red Shirt's wife," she said politely in introduction. Her arms suddenly felt very empty. Red Shirt had Junior, she'd have to let his father give him a new, better name; and Prudence was holding Baby Brother, Big Sister cuddled next to her. "So, why do you want to be here?" she asked brusquely, her tone changing with the subconscious threat of another adult woman in the tribe, stealing the attentions of her newfound family.

"Well," Prudence started, feeling uncomfortable with the direct cross-examination she was getting from a white woman who appeared to be about ten years her junior. "I, um, well, I wasn't happy."

Rachel gave her a snort and a sharp stare: what difference does that make? Isn't that how life is most of the time?

Prudence saw 'the look' and changed approaches. "My father was very controlling. I was, am, ugly and no man wanted to marry me. So, my father was going to pay this pig of a person to be my husband. He was fat and ugly and rude and when my father wasn't looking, he'd grab me. 'Ooh, nice bosoms,' he'd say or pat my bottom and tell me that I was sweeter than a two dollar whore. He had red bumpy spots on his arms and face. My father said that I shouldn't pay them any mind. After all, I had this one big one on mine," she said as she touched the birthmark that covered a large part of the left side of her face.

Rachel listened but didn't comment. She knew there was more to the story. "My father insisted that I marry Sylvester. I didn't want to, really I didn't. I knew, sort of, what a man did to a woman after they were married. He told me not to worry about that even though I never brought up the subject. He wanted to talk about it all the time—he was obsessed with it. 'You see,' he said, 'I wanted to make sure I knew how to pleasure my wife so I've been going to the whorehouses since I was yay high,'" Prudence quoted in a squeaky voice, and then indicated a youthful height. "He said he knew all about," she shook her head in disgust, "all the places he could put his prick to make me happy." She shuddered in recollection. "Daddy didn't believe me when I told him about the way he talked to me. He said that I had to do what my husband told me to, that I shouldn't be so picky because I was so ugly, and that I should be happy that a nice gentleman like Sylvester was willing to make me his wife."

Baby Brother started squirming in her arms as she attempted to finish her story. "Here," Rachel said and took him from her. "It's his bedtime," then bared her breast to feed him.

She gave Rachel the baby, grateful for the break in her story. She didn't like thinking about Sylvester or her father, but she needed to explain to this young woman why she didn't want to go back. Maybe she could convince her husband to let her stay. But, whether she could or couldn't, Rachel could probably ask him 'not' to let her stay. Two arguing women in one house, or small tribe, would make life miserable for everyone.

"You have a beautiful son," Prudence praised as Rachel settled herself, now ready to resume the conversation.

"He's not my son, he's Number Two's. Big Sister here is his daughter, too. Their mother died while he was out hunting. I'm feeding him until he's old enough for big people food. That's my husband and my son," she said as she nodded to Red Shirt, playing his poke and tease reflex game with his charge. "We were just married a couple of days ago. He's a good man. So, did Sylvester hit you?" she asked sincerely—she was starting to like Prudence. There had to be another reason why she wasn't willing to marry the man.

"No, he just touched me where I didn't want to be touched," she answered. Rachel nodded that she knew how that felt but didn't interrupt. "But his spots: I knew what they were. He had syphilis. I read about the symptoms in a book. I told him I thought that was why he had the bumps. He got mad, real mad. He said I'd better not tell my Daddy about it. Anyway, he said it was a lie. He said that some of the whores he'd been with had it, but that he couldn't get it. He was imbued or commune or something—I forget the word. Anyway, it's like if you had the measles once, you'd never get them again."

Big Sister inhaled sharply then brought her knees up to her chest in fear. She didn't understand much of what the women were talking about, but she did know the word measles. She pointed to Prudence and asked, "Measles?"

"Oh, no, no, no, sweetheart," she said and gathered the frightened girl close, rocking her like the young child she was. "No measles, no diseases of any kind. I'm very healthy. I just look funny and I'm a bit old."

"So you don't have the pox," Rachel asked Prudence. She shook her head and held Big Sister even closer. She had always wanted a daughter and now that she felt the young girl in her arms, her desire for one was even stronger. She looked up and smiled at Number Two, the girl's father. He was nice to look at, strong, and, she sighed, he didn't cringe when he looked at her.

Number Two watched the women as they talked together. He was glad that they let Big Sister stay with them. She had been very close to her mother and missed her terribly. Now there was at least one good woman in their tribe who she could learn from. Maybe two. He had seen the large mark on the new white woman's face but that didn't bother him. He had one on his belly and it didn't make him different from any other man. She was nice to his daughter, had held her as if she was her own, and smiled at his son, too. It would be good if she had milk to feed his son—then he would take her for sure. But, she had let Rachel feed Baby Brother. He sighed. Even if she didn't have milk, he'd like to keep her.

"I'm sorry," Prudence apologized and looked away from the handsome brave back to her confidant. Rachel had been speaking to her and she wasn't paying attention. "I didn't hear you."

"Would you keep him here with you tonight? You can sleep here and if he wakes up, just bring him to me and I'll feed him. I want to sleep with my husband and son," Rachel said, the unmistakable grin of anticipation of lovemaking showing across her whole, slightly twitching body.

"Sure, but if you think that Big Sister and I can handle both of them, you can leave your son here, too. I don't know how it is to lie with a husband, but I think it might be nicer if you didn't have a wee one right next to you." Prudence didn't have any personal experience, but Sylvester had gone on and on about what a husband and wife did when they were married. Some of it had to be true.

"Wow, thank you. That would be nice. I'll just go feed Juni..." Rachel bit off the name. This was their new life. She would not use that name again. She'd have to remember to ask Marty not to use it either. "I'll feed my son and bring him over here in a little bit," she said then took her leave.

Number Two watched as his daughter tried to communicate with Prudence, the woman who did not like her name. He'd give her another one if she stayed.

Baby Brother had fallen asleep and now Big Sister was running her fingers through the white woman's hair, getting ready to plait it like her own. There were very few words between them but they seemed to understand each other. And, like each other. There would never be anyone like his first wife, but he could have a new one. He could make good memories with her. And, make more children, too.

Rachel walked over to Prudence, her slumbering son in her arms. "Here, he fell asleep already," she said, then lay him down gently on the little bed that Big Sister had prepared, hoping that he'd stay asleep. "I guess the potato he ate for dinner agreed with him. I'll just be over there," Rachel pointed to the private area near the food cache. "Thanks again. And these men are nicer than any white men I've ever met. Be good to them and they'll be good to you. Oh, and Marty and I aren't prisoners. We're here because we choose to be."

Big Sister settled the two boys together then curled around the pair, keeping them warm with her body heat, her back to the fire. It felt so good to have a full belly. *Pfrat!* But those potatoes gave her gas.

Prudence saw that the sleeping pallet Big Sister had set up for her was in between the cozy little baby boys' nest and one other. She looked over coyly to see if her suspicions were correct. Number Two was still watching her. He appeared to be the only one who hadn't claimed his spot. Maybe he was the sentinel tonight. Marty wasn't there yet but the bedroll on the other side of the fire looked like a white man's, not an Indian's. Rachel and Red Shirt were in their 'suite' near the food cache, already making soft, happy noises. Yes, the bed next to hers was most likely Number Two's. She glanced over in his direction again, this time feeling brave enough to smile at him. She rearranged her skirts and got ready to lie back. Her hands reached up and felt the two braids Big Sister had put in her hair. A warm glow covered her body—she was starting to feel like an Indian already.

Number Two made his decision. He came to his conclusion with the big head on his shoulders, but he had to admit, it was also influenced by the little head in his breechclout. He'd see if the woman would lie with him tonight. The near fight with Red Shirt earlier made it clear to him that having only one young woman between the two adult braves was dangerous. It was even worse because Rachel was so close to his son. He was grateful that she could give him her milk, but watching her feed his child stirred up feelings that he shouldn't have for another man's wife. He was grateful that Dances Naked had interceded in the misunderstanding even if it wasn't his family involved. No, the white man was a part of their family now. He had been clever and generous in getting food for them. He would always be a member of his tribe, his family.

Number Two walked over to the fire and thrust the end of his pitch soaked stick into the flame, twisting it around to catch fire. He was sure the new woman was still watching him. He didn't want her to go to sleep yet. He had something to show her. He stood back and waved the torch at the woman who did not like her name, to show her he wanted her to come away with him.

"Okay," she said pensively then nodded to make sure he understood she'd come with him. Rachel had said these were good men; she'd have to trust her new friend's judgment.

The quiet young father led her thirty feet away from the campfire then handed her the torch. "Thank you," she said nervously, not knowing what to expect but wanting to say something.

The brave bent sideways and pulled out the knot in the leather thong holding up his breechclout. He held his clothing in place; he didn't want to scare her by giving her the wrong impression. But, she wasn't frightened, not much anyway. She looked into his face, trying to read his intentions. What she saw wasn't threatening; he meant her no harm.

He could see that she wasn't afraid of him. He was glad that she trusted him already. He sighed loudly then pulled out the leather belt and let his breechclout drop to the ground. His shirt was long and covered him. Hopefully, she wouldn't think he was there to take her against her will.

Prudence didn't take her eyes off Number Two's face. She knew he was taking off his pants, as they were, but could see that he wasn't aggressive. He gently guided her torch bearing hand down toward his groin. He lifted his shirt to the side with one hand and pointed with the other: he wanted her to see it.

Prudence was bashful and didn't want to look down, "Umph," he grunted, as he looked her in the eye then peered down to where he wanted her to look. She let her eyes follow his gaze then saw it: the port wine stain birthmark just like hers, only lower, much lower. It didn't cover his privates but was off to the side.

His hand was covering the area that he would only share with his wife. He left his hand there then reached up with the other, the one he had been pointing with, and gently touched the deep reddish purple side of her face. Yes, it felt just like the rest of her skin, just like the skin on one side of his lower belly felt like the other.

"Thank you," she said softly, placing her hand on top of his cheek-caressing palm. "You're beautiful, too."

Number Two inhaled deeply. He wanted to be with her tonight, to join with her, and make her his wife. She was beautiful despite the berry-colored skin on her face, and she smelled like springtime. He dropped his other hand, letting the shirt hide his man parts that were beginning to swell with happiness and hope—he didn't want to scare her. She looked older, as old as he was, and much older than Rachel, but she also looked pure. He would be gentle with her, take his time, and guide her so she would enjoy becoming one with him. The night was long. They would have time. Hopefully, the children wouldn't waken.

"I think we should go back," Prudence said as she looked back to the campfire and the others who were now filling in the empty spaces. Marty had thrown out his blanket and was trying to cover his bare legs by pulling the edges up over them. Just as he got one side arranged, the other would fall down. He groaned in frustration and decided to sleep on his side. Red Shirt was already with Rachel. They both could hear her giggles and the chief's short, abbreviated grunts of satisfaction.

Number Two took her free hand into his, squatted down quickly, and retrieved his leather belt and breechclout with the other. He should put it on before going to his bed but he didn't want to dress in front of her. Yes, he'd let her keep the torch and lead the way to their adjoining beds.

Prudence put the torch into the fire and walked to the pallet that Big Sister had prepared for her. Number Two kept hold of her hand as she settled onto it. Or maybe she kept hold of his hand as she lay down. No, they were both holding onto each other, even though it was awkward. Neither one of them wanted to be the first to let go.

Finally, Number Two released her hand, but only so he could scoot his bedroll closer to hers. Prudence rolled onto her side, trying not to listen, sort of, to the sounds of lovemaking from Rachel and her Indian brave. It wouldn't take much, maybe, to begin a relationship with Number Two. She already knew that he liked her. She knew that a man's member got bigger when it was time to mate. Sylvester had grabbed her hand once and put it on his crotch. 'This is for you,' he had said, then gyrated underneath her trapped palm. She shuddered at the memory.

The woman must be cold—she is shaking. Number Two scooted closer to her and put his arm over her waist, pulling her gently to him so she could share his warmth. He could smell her. She smelled of the flowers in the spring, the pink ones with thorns on them that bloomed for less than a month, and then were gone. Her hair was parted; Big Sister had plaited her hair and now her neck and shoulders were bare. Without thinking, his nose moved in to her neck, sniffing gently so he could get more of her aroma. He felt her react with a quick gasp. But, she didn't move away. It took a moment, but she responded to him. She took her hand, placed it on his arm, then scooted as close to him as she could with her clothes on. Number Two gulped. She had her clothes on. He wanted them off but his daughter was on the other side of the woman he wanted to mate with. He was fairly sure that she felt the same way about him but he knew that the first time, if it was her first time, they should be alone. She would have some pain and he didn't want her to cry out and scare the children.

Ж

Red Shirt let Rachel fall asleep after they had become one again. Tonight she had asked him to give the boy a name. "Later," he had told her, glad that he could remember the word to use. It was easier for him to understand the white man's words than to speak them.

"Later?" she asked then tilted her head aside; her eyes squinted as if picturing that name applied to her toddler son. He shook his head and snorted in negation. "Oh," she said as realization hit her, "you'll give him a name, later…"

He nodded. Yes, she was pretty and soft and tasted good all over; could cook potatoes, and was nice to the other children, but she wasn't too bright. But, she was his…and so was the boy.

He was tired but needed to stay awake and make sure Number Two didn't mate with the white woman who had walked into their village. She had a family and they would be looking for her. Yes, he would have to make sure they stayed apart. Big Sister had put the woman who did not like her name's bed between her and her father. He wouldn't embarrass the man by moving it away from her. But, he would make sure they kept their clothes on.

The woman was older. Maybe she had a husband before and he had died. Maybe she had children and they were dead also. Maybe—but she was alone now. If they joined tonight and his seed overtook hers, she could not go back to her family. The white man would hunt down his people if she came back with an Indian child in her belly. He knew this. He had seen it happen. He wouldn't let it happen to his brother-in-law.

Ж

Number Two awoke before anyone. He hadn't joined with the woman, but now wished he had. She probably would have been able to be quiet and not cry out in pain when her maidenhead was pierced, but it was too late now. The sun would be rising soon. If he had made her his wife, Red Shirt wouldn't be able to send her away. Now he could. But, before she left, he would give her a gift: a name. He leaned forward and gave her a kiss on her pale, soft neck. She sighed and her bottom squirmed toward him in response to his lips. Then she froze. She panicked momentarily when she felt it: his firmness. She realized what it was and who it belonged to then relaxed back into it, wiggling against him as if was the cure to the itch she felt deep inside her womb. Oh wait—it *was* the solution.

Number Two's arm reached over her waist and pointed to the sky just above the horizon. She followed his finger and saw what he was pointing to. "You," he said in a guttural tone.

"The Morning Star?" she whispered. "You mean I'm the Morning Star?" Number Two nodded and smiled although she wasn't looking at him. He kissed her neck again, making himself even more uncomfortable with the feel of her closeness. "My name is Morning Star?" she asked, then turned over to face him, her hand on his waist for reassurance.

"Morning Star, beautiful," he replied. She was a woman and he could speak English with her, when they were in private.

"Thank you," she said then leaned forward to place her face close to his. She'd never kissed a man—Daddy didn't count and his kisses were always on the cheek anyhow. She shut her eyes, waited, and then felt his nose touching hers, rubbing against hers softly, letting his lips brush hers. The gentle brushing continued until she couldn't hold back. She smashed her lips into his as she reached around his waist and clutched him tightly to her. She wasn't sure what was happening: it had to be instinct. All she knew was that she wanted to tear off her clothes and rub her skin all over his. His mouth was on hers, but she wanted to be inside his mouth. And, she wanted that prick part to be inside her, too.

Number Two pulled away quickly and sharply, pushed her away, then got to his feet. No words were spoken, but suddenly a foot was kicking her.

Red Shirt had found them in their tangled limb embrace and had kicked Number Two away from her, accidentally kicking her, too. He shook his head at her then glared at Number Two: no mating.

The scuffle had awakened Marty and now the others were rousing, too. Rachel stepped over her son and reached for Baby Brother who was gnawing at his fist, getting ready to waken everyone. Oops—too late! Marty looked around and saw that there was trouble in paradise. Red Shirt was on the warpath with Number Two again. At least this time it didn't involve Rachel.

"What's going on?" Prudence asked Marty.

"Well, I don't speak Cherokee or whatever it is they're speaking, but I think that Number Two wasn't supposed to, um, be familiar with you last night. You were supposed to go back to your family untouched."

"But I don't want to go back!" she carped. "I like it here and I like him, too. I want to be his wife!" she said, then added, "And, I'm pretty sure he wants me, too!"

"Well, if Red Shirt stopped you two in time, then he'll send you back," Marty said plainly, trying to hold back the feeling of dejection that he was sharing with her.

"And if he didn't?" Prudence asked vehemently, shoulders back in defiance. She was upset about the leaving part, but was also suffering from a severe case of *coitus interuptus*.

"Well, they can't chance you going back pregnant," Marty began then stopped. He could see the plan forming in her head. She'd lie—say anything—to stay. He was a light sleeper and knew they hadn't consummated their hoped for relationship. He wouldn't rat them out though. He doubted if he could anyway. He'd seen that determined look before. She'd stay with Number Two if she had to sew herself to him.

Prudence interrupted the two men's argument, not with words, but with her attitude. She bent over and picked up the breechclout Number Two had never put back on. She waved it at Red Shirt then took solid, stomping footsteps to her betrothed, putting her arm inside his elbow. She handed him his loincloth, which he accepted with a slight smirk. She pointed to her birthmark then pointed down to the part of his shirt that covered

137

the mark Number Two had shown her earlier. "Mine," she said, then hugged his arm closer to her.

Number Two's grin grew in pride at his clever wife's declaration. She hadn't lied to the chief, that would have been bad, but she had let him assume that they had mated. He could claim her as his wife now, but they'd have to wait until evening to seal their union. And, maybe they would make another son for him.

14 One More for the Tribe

Fortunately, the morning confrontation ended without blows being thrown or anyone being evicted from the tribe—at least not yet. Marty knew that Red Shirt had a difficult decision to make—keep Prudence or escort her home. He was a newlywed himself and surely didn't begrudge his second in command a wife and mother for his two young, motherless children. It wasn't an easy issue to resolve, but it just got harder. It looked like the two new acquaintances had really hit it off and sealed the bond of marriage. Red Shirt couldn't let her go back to her father if she was possibly carrying Number Two's baby. Her father certainly wouldn't believe how she was wantonly throwing herself at the Indian brave. He was sure to claim rape and want revenge. No, Marty decided—it wasn't going to be a hard choice for the chief. She would have to stay with them and hope that her father believed her tale of going to England.

Red Shirt hadn't meant to fall asleep after making love to his wife. But, they had made love nearly all night long the night before and were both tired. He should have asked The Young One to watch out for them. No, it was his responsibility and he had failed. Deep down, he was happy it had happened though. He knew how the hole in his life was filled by the warm love and nearness of his new wife and their son. Number Two's loss was fresher, but still just as painful. Now they would both have wives and their tribe would grow again.

Ж

The new white woman made her one word claim of Number Two, "Mine," then waited silently by his side; chin out in pride as she locked arms with her new husband. Red Shirt sighed at his lieutenant, pointed to the breechclout, and flicked his fingers in a sweeping motion: 'get your pants on, man.'

Number Two stepped behind some bushes for discretion and returned, chest puffed out, his eyes fixed on the chief: 'I await your command.' Red Shirt grunted and the two walked away as if nothing had happened, leaving the breakfast meal to the women.

"I've got a pan for porritch," Prudence said to Rachel, who was nursing Baby Brother. "Should I go ahead and get it started. I mean, I don't know how this is supposed to work. It was just my Daddy and me, and I did everything when it came to cooking. You'll probably have your arms full of babies all the time, and well, I'd just like to make this as fair as possible."

Rachel shook her head. "I never thought that I'd be sharing my life with a good man much less another woman, or anyone, who wanted to be fair and make life easier for me. Yes, I'd appreciate it if you took over the cooking duties, at least until one of these little men are weaned. Oh, and congratulations; I think you got a good man, too."

"Do you need a hand there, Prudence?" Marty asked as he walked up to the little kitchen area.

The woman bowed her head and blushed, then looked up and answered him. "No, thank you, I can handle this, and you're welcome to stay and visit but, um," she fumbled awkwardly for the words to use, "my name isn't Prudence anymore: it's Morning Star."

"It is? That's a beautiful name!" Marty declared. "Did your husband give it to you?"

If Morning Star had been blushing before, she was positively scarlet now, her redness blending into her wine-colored birthmark. Rather than speak, she nodded her head, her embarrassment quickly turning into pride. She had a husband now. She was the head cook and not a stranger nor a runaway woman. It was going to be a long day, but she knew that when nighttime came, she would have her wedding night and officially become Number Two's wife.

Ж

"I hate to bother you, but when do you think we can head out to The Trees?" Marty asked Red Shirt when they were alone, the two of them hauling in long lengths of fallen trees to turn into building timbers.

Red Shirt heard him, even knew the meaning of every word he was saying, but didn't reply. Maybe if he ignored him, he'd quit asking. Maybe, but not likely.

"Ahem, ahem," Marty cleared his throat loudly. Red Shirt cut his eyes over to the insistent white man. He might as well pay attention to him now or he'd never leave him alone. He put down the tree and stood up straight to face the man's question.

Marty gulped when he realized how much of a pest he must seem. There was a lot of work to do and Red Shirt wanted to get it done. "I know you have to build homes for your family and the rest of the tribe," Marty said and pointed his right hand over to indicate the people, "but if you could see fit to just take a couple of days out of your time to get me at least headed in the right direction, I'd really appreciate it. I really, really want to get back to my wife and son as soon as possible," he explained, again using his air drawn curvy woman and cradled baby sign language, unintentionally ending his plea with a stuck out bottom lip and a sniffle.

Red Shirt sighed deeply. It was the same story, just told on a different day. If he didn't give him some answer, he'd hear the plea again tonight, tomorrow morning and on and on until he did have the time to lead him to those bad medicine trees. Red Shirt pointed to the clear sky, then the storm-killed tree they were hauling back to camp, then over to the woods where he would find more timber to bring in. He brought one hand up above his head and wafted his fingers down to indicate snowflakes, then cupped them together upside down to form a house. He finished his answer with a head shake, no, and then gave him the sign for a home four more times. They needed to build five homes before he would lead him to where he wanted to go.

"Five," Marty said with a grimace as he held up his opened hand, displaying all fingers and thumb. "Five homes and then you'll take me to see my family?" Marty asked, although he was sure that's what Red Shirt was trying to tell him.

Red Shirt nodded curtly, then bent down and picked up his lumber source. He had 'spoken' and now it was time to get to work. It was late summer, but they should have time to get all of their homes built now that they didn't have to go hunting. It was too late to plant any crops, but they could clear some land after their homes were built. And, if Dances Naked stayed, he'd probably help with the work. He was old and a white man, but still an asset to his tribe. And, he was also smart and knew that the sooner the tribe's chores were done, the sooner he would get back to his wife and son.

15 Little Bear

Winter was still several months away, but Little Bear wanted to scout out his new trapping territory early. He knew the local fur trader would know if someone else was already working the area. Michael Huntsman was a decent man although usually a bit too tightfisted in his bargaining. It wasn't that he was mean or cheap—he just liked to talk. The longer he could haggle over a good price for his foodstuffs against the pelts, the longer he could visit and socialize.

Little Bear had traded with Michael for three years now and was looking forward to seeing him again. Well, not exactly Michael—he was eager to see if his daughter, Prudence, was still single. He didn't know if she was timid or just being respectful of her father's business when she stayed in the background while they negotiated prices. She never said much, but did seem to know the value of furs and which ones were in demand as well as her father did.

Yes, he would like to see her and that sweet smile that peeked out from under her oversized mobcap again. Maybe he'd have enough nerve to ask for her hand this year. It could be that it was too much to hope that a bright woman like her would want to live a rugged life with someone like him—an outcast British doctor who dressed, acted, and spoke like an Indian. But, that was who he was and, no matter how bright and appealing a woman was, he wasn't going to change for her or anyone else. He had tried that once and it didn't turn out very well. But, coming to America was a good choice, even if it hadn't been his decision to make.

However, that was years ago and now he was embarking on a new season in his career of choice. Yes, Michael's store wasn't exactly on his way to his new trapping grounds, but he did need supplies and still had a few prime, tanned beaver furs left to barter for winter supplies. And, he still had a glimmer of hope that he'd leave with a wife, too.

Ж

He smelled him before he heard the grunts, moans, and snorts. Little Bear was downwind of a man who couldn't make up his mind on whether to cry, curse, or chuckle. He quickly tied up his mules and hurried closer for a better look at the source of the fecal stench and mercurial moods.

And, there he was, buried up to his neck with large stones, pebbles, and dirt, a rough sliver of wood just out of reach of his mouth. It appeared that he had been using the little scrap as a shovel to move the smaller pieces of rock and rubble away from his face. Little Bear shook his head—there was no way he was going to disinter the man. This was obviously an Indian form of punishment or death. The Cherokees around here wouldn't torture anyone just for fun; this man must have deserved it.

Little Bear watched as the man stretched and strained, finally sticking out his tongue far enough that he was able to urge the wooden pick to his mouth. He wrapped his lips around it, and then started flinging pebbles away from his neck, pausing after a couple of minutes to pant and curse through teeth clenched tightly around his treasured stick. He wasn't going to let loose of his improvised tool again.

Just as he was leaving, Little Bear remembered where he had smelled that stench and heard that whiny voice. This was the man who had beaten his little sister about the head and shoulders six, or was it seven, years ago. "Hmph," Little Bear snorted, not caring whether he was heard of not. That monster child-beater definitely deserved his punishment, if not for what he did to anger the Cherokee, then for the way he had pummeled his little sister.

He should have hit him harder and spared the Indians the inconvenience. At least she was away from him now—hopefully, she was safe.

Ж

"Hey, there, Little Bear!" Michael called out. "What did you bring me?"

Little Bear smiled at his friend, happy that the old man was still here. He looked around casually as he scanned the area for Prudence, and remarked, "Doesn't look like anything's changed."

"Well, the house and store are the same, but there's just me here now," he replied.

Michael was waiting for Little Bear to ask where Prudence was, but the trapper wasn't biting. He knew chatty Michael would tell him soon enough.

And, he did. "Ye see, my daughter, Prudence, ye remember her, aye?"

"Aye," Little Bear answered, hoping he'd get to the point right away.

"Weel, ye see, she always wanted to go to England to see the castles and churches and such. She has kin there, her Uncle Remus. He told her that she was welcome there anytime and I guess she thought that now was a good time. I was disappointed though. I had a fine husband picked out for her: Sylvester, the blacksmith over at Chapel Hill. But she didn't care for him. She said that those red bumps all over his skin was the pox. Hmph! She coulda stayed here and had a good husband. He'd treat her nice, never beat her, give her lots of pretty things, but she'd rather go gallivantin' off to see her Uncle." Michael shook his head in frustration. "Now, enough about her—what did ye bring me?"

Little Bear showed him the top grade beaver pelts that he had tanned over the summer, the ones he had held back to give a bride if he could find one. But, it looked like the only single woman who interested him was thousands of miles away in the country he had promised himself he would never return to.

The only other woman who had turned his head was married: Evie. She was with child when they parted ways last year. Surely, she'd delivered her baby without a problem, but she may not have been able to keep her husband, or keep him alive. Ian had sworn vengeance on the men who had captured and tortured him. He hadn't said he was leaving Evie, but Little Bear could see that a wife and child didn't fit into Ian's retaliation plans. But, Evie was sure to be all right: she had her husband's Uncle Jody and Aunt Sarah to watch over her. Hmm, it was quite possible that she was now a single woman—widowed or otherwise. Maybe he'd go back to the Pomeroy's place next spring and see. Maybe he could get a wife and a child at the same time.

Ж

Little Bear knew that if he had been willing to stay longer, he could have bargained for more food. But, even though he rushed the transaction, he had managed to get plenty of cornmeal, salt, coffee, a couple rashers of bacon, and a bag of dried apples for the beaver furs. He waited until Michael thought they were done then brought out the flawless mink fur.

"I guess I won't be needin' a ham for a wedding dinner after all," Michael said as he offered Little Bear the smoked meat as a trade for the mink, his only good deal of the day. "I still have a couple of other small hams that'll last me quite a while." He purred as he stroked the ultra-soft pelt, "Ah, I always did want a mink pillow cover."

Of course, the information that no one had been trapping due west was just what the trapper had wanted to hear. He'd head out there right now and see the river up close while it was still summer. It was easier to see the best places to set up traps and cross the water now, before snowfall hid the landscape.

It was late when he left Michael's—too late to do anything but find a place to spend the night. He traveled an hour, found a clearing with large boulders scattered about, and decided to set up camp there. He could climb on top of the highest pile of stones and see the shortest route to the river. It was approaching dusk and he needed to survey the area before he lost his last bit of daylight; the mules could stay loaded a few minutes longer. He looked down as he started to scale the first in the series of stair stepping boulders and saw it: cornmeal bits and hoof and shoe prints. It looked like a woman's shoe had tried to erase the traces of cornmeal and hoof prints on the ground. Why would a woman, any woman, be out here? It had to be a white woman, too, because squaws didn't wear shoes with heels. And, these were most likely Indian ponies that had passed through—they weren't shod.

Little Bear looked at his mules then at the stones: they needed a break and the view of the trail would still be there in the morning. The skies were clear and the trail of the woman following the Indian ponies would be no harder to follow tomorrow than it was now. He sighed and shook his head as he started unpacking the mules. "Time for dinner, girls; we can deal with this conundrum in the morning. It's been a long day."

Ж

If he hadn't stopped where he did, he probably wouldn't have seen the trail. Yes, the woman, or very small-footed man, had done a fair job of obscuring the trail of cornmeal, but once he had seen it, he knew what to look for. Of course, he erased the clues as he followed them. If Michael wanted to believe that his daughter had gone to England, he'd let him. Prudence was a bright girl and, by the look of disappointment in the old man's face as he related the tale of the unrequited arranged marriage, he would bet that the smart woman had fashioned her own escape. Hopefully, she was safe. But, she was wise and wouldn't take off without a destination and a plan. "Hmph," he remarked, spooking the mules that weren't used to hearing him speak. "Now I'm curious."

Ж

The wind carried the smell of beans cooking toward him. He followed the smell—it was actually easier to track than the footprints. His mystery person had wisely avoided walking over the dusty areas and hadn't left an easy trail. Now that he could track with his nose up in the air rather than with his eyes down to the ground, he saw her.

Or rather, them. The two white women, both of them toting babies in slings fashioned from torn petticoats, were gathering wood from outside the Indian settlement. "Hallo, there," he called out, hoping that he didn't frighten them or their men.

"Little Bear?" she asked, one part of her hoping that it was him, another part fearing it.

"Prudence?" he answered. Now that he heard her voice, he was sure that it was she, although the Indian baby she held close couldn't be hers. She had only been gone a few days according to what Michael had said.

"Not anymore," she answered. "My name is Morning Star. What brings you here," she asked suspiciously.

"Your name is Little Bear?" asked the young mother with the older, and obviously white, baby.

"Yes, they call me Little Bear. Do I know you?" he asked. She seemed familiar but he couldn't place where or when he had seen her.

"I never knew your name. I'm Rachel and you, um, beat the 'tar' out of my brother a few years ago. I never got the chance to thank you. You see, he never hit me in the face again after the thrashing you gave him. And, he'll never hit me again, anywhere, ever again. So, what are you doing here and how come you know Morning Star?"

"I guess I'm a little lost," Little Bear said with a big grin. This was the first time he had seen Michael's daughter without the oversized hat. Now he knew why she always wore it: she had been hiding the large birthmark on the side of her face. It didn't diminish her beauty though. She looked so right with a baby on her hip. He realized he was musing and started again. "I mean, I didn't think I'd come all the way to England. At least, that's where Mr. Huntsman said his daughter went."

Morning Star paled, fear overcoming her momentary elation at seeing the familiar face of the handsome, good mannered trapper. "Don't worry," Little Bear said. "I'm only joking. Your father was disappointed that you left for England, but it's where you wanted to be, and he accepted it. I won't tell him any differently. Looks like you found some family here, too."

The women turned around as their husbands rushed to them, followed by Marty who was shouting, "It's okay. I'm sure it's okay!"

The two men grabbed their women and sons close to them and stared at the strange white man dressed in Indian clothing, his long blond streaked, wavy hair pulled back into a single, long braid. Little Bear greeted them in their own tongue, and told them that he was a visitor to this area and hoped to be able to do some trapping nearby. He wouldn't bother their hunting and would be respectful of their village and its people.

Marty couldn't understand what they were saying but saw the sincerity in the stranger's eyes. He could also tell that he knew the women. He waited until the men were finished speaking, or at least paused, then jumped in and introduced himself. "Hi, I'm Marty Melbourne, and these are my friends. Well, we're almost family, at least until I can get back to my own, which I hope is very soon," he said, then cut his eyes over to Red Shirt. He air drew his wife and cradled his invisible son, then grinned at the chief: I'll never stop asking for them, he signed, then added a smirk. "I take it you know Red Shirt's and Number Two's wives?" he asked.

"Yes, I knew these women in their past lives," Little Bear answered, hoping that he was being politically correct. He looked to the Indian men and repeated himself in Cherokee. He wanted them to know what he was saying, and to make sure they understood that they needn't fear him, that he wasn't trying to take away their women or make trouble for them. He also knew he didn't need to explain; they appeared to be sharp men and probably understood English, too.

Marty opened his mouth, ready to invite the new man to dinner, but chomped down on his first words, "If you're hungry," knowing that it wasn't his place to invite the visitor to a meal. That was Red Shirt's duty or responsibility, depending on how he felt about the man.

"Little Bear saved me from my brother," Rachel told her husband, mimicking the punches to her face that had stopped because of him. "I only lost the one tooth," she said and pointed to her one missing lower tooth. "I would've lost them all if 'he' had kept hitting me in the face." She'd never use her brother's given name again and didn't want to hear anyone else say it either. She shook her head as she recalled the event years ago. "I'm sure glad you came around that day," she said.

Red Shirt glanced at his wife then at Little Bear. Little Bear put his hand down to indicate the size she was when he had intervened. Red Shirt nodded his head; he understood and thanked him. Then he grinned, recalling how he had punished her brother.

Little Bear saw the grin and knew that he was the one who had buried the man he had come upon the day before. He nodded back and grinned just as big, hoping that Rachel's husband understood that he had seen his handiwork.

"What's going on—did I miss something?" Marty asked. These two men, now three with Number Two joining the unspoken conversation, were nodding and grinning. Well, whatever it was, no one was throwing fists or angry words.

"So, are you going to be trapping near here?" Morning Star asked, hoping to change the subject to one that was audible and that she understood.

"Far enough away so I won't be bothering you and your, um, family," Little Bear answered, hoping that she would explain her relationship.

"Oh, Number Two here is my husband now," she said, her face radiant at recalling how they had become married. "And he was widowed so now I have a daughter, yay high," she said indicating her height with her hand, "and a son." She lifted up Baby Brother so Little Bear could get a closer look at the handsome boy, happily gnawing a strip of leather thong.

"You know, um, Morning Star," he fumbled, "if your husband and the others trap and get more than they need, I'll stop by here next spring and take the furs to your father and get what you need in the way of supplies. He won't know that you're here. I mean, Marty said he was leaving, and I really don't believe your men will get as much for their furs as a, um, white man," he said, embarrassed at calling himself a white man. He sighed then repeated himself in Cherokee although, by the shocked then happy look on Red Shirt's face, he already understood. He'd have to make sure he didn't say anything to Morning Star in English that he didn't want the braves to hear, too.

Ж

Red Shirt wound up inviting Little Bear to a dinner of beans with a slice of ham fat added for flavoring. He excused himself after the meal, letting his host know that he wanted to continue on to his trapping grounds. He didn't need to repeat that he wouldn't let anyone know he had come upon the white women who were now wives in the tribe; it was understood.

But, he didn't want to stay the night with the tribe who, except for the colorful and cranky old women, slept under the stars. No, he didn't want to be sleeping next to two newlywed couples. Especially since one of the wives, the woman formerly known as Prudence, the bright but bashful woman who he should have asked to marry him the year before, was one of the new brides.

"One of these days," he said softly to his mule as he led her away from the camp, "one of these days, I'll have a woman of my own."

16 Milk and Cookies

Against all financial and common sense, Little Bear made a detour to civilization rather than head directly to investigate his new trapping grounds. He couldn't explain it, but ever since he had seen the two young couples and their babies, he had a bad case of Daddy lust. Or husband lust. Or just plain lust. He wanted a woman, but not in the worst way—he wanted one in the best way. He never thought that he, with his rough and chilly trapper's lifestyle, was good enough for a wife. Last year after he saw how happy Evie was with absolutely no worldly possessions, not even a dress, he realized that it wasn't the solid structure of a house a woman needed, but a loving and supportive man. Prudence, a lovely, intelligent woman with nice clothes and well-read by the books he had seen at her father's trading post, was just as unlikely a candidate for a primitive, wet and often cold, outdoors life. But, from the moment he had seen them, he could tell that both women were happy in their rustic existence.

Yes, maybe a detour to the Pomeroy's homestead was in order. Jody would know where Evie was. She had lived without a house the winter before he met her and maybe, if Ian had met with tragedy in his vengeance quest and she was now widowed, she would be willing to return to the wilds with him as her husband. All of the sudden, he wanted the mules to travel faster and for longer hours. It felt great to have a personal quest rather than a quota of pelts to pursue.

Ж

"Mommy, Mommy, there's a man coming to see you," Jenny screamed as she ran up the porch steps.

"Hold on there," I said as I braced her by the shoulders to let her catch her breath. "Where is he and did he ask for me by name?" No man had ever called on me that I could recall. "Are you sure he isn't here for your father or Grandpa Jody or your Grannie?"

"Nope," she replied just a little too quickly. She looked around the room, avoiding my eyes, but also looking for something. "Can I give him a cookie?" she asked.

"Who is he?" I asked. Something wasn't right or she wouldn't be so quiet and evasive.

"I think his name is Small Bear," she answered hesitantly then looked back at the plate of cookies.

"Jennnny..." I dragged out her name, giving her the opportunity to explain herself.

"He didn't tell me his name," she admitted, "but I know it's something like Small Bear. I, um, well, I just know it is. Can I give him a cookie? He's a nice man and he and his mules have come a long way to get here. He's a trapper!" she crowed, happy that I wasn't upset with her.

"You know things early, don't you, dear?" I asked. My eldest daughter, Leah, also had 'the sight,' the sixth sense, good old ESP. Jenny was my adopted daughter and I had suspected she had it on at least two previous occasions. This was the first time I had asked her about it though. I didn't know if she even knew she had it.

Jenny shrugged her shoulders. Knowing things early was natural for her. She had tried telling her brothers, her other brothers from her first family who were dead now, about it but they wouldn't believe her. She never spoke of it again until today.

"Small Bear?" I paused. "Do you mean Little Bear?" I asked, excited about the possibility of seeing the first friend I had met in this 18th century.

"That's it! He's almost here! I'll take him some water, and can he have two cookies? It's been a long time since he's had one, um, I'm pretty sure. I mean, he's a trapper and I don't think they bake very many cookies."

"Let's just start with one, okay? Now, let me make sure the wee three are still asleep. Oops, too late. Wren's up and now her brothers are, too."

"Mommy, can I take Wren and the cookie and you can take my brothers?" Jenny asked. "He already has water, but I'm sure he'd like to come in and sit down for a while. He's a nice man, huh, Mommy?" Jenny asked although I was sure that she already knew the answer.

"Yes, dear. Come on kids; let's go meet Uncle Little Bear. He knew about you even before I did."

Ж

I didn't know if Little Bear had stumbled on a rock when he saw me or if he really was so shocked that he almost fainted. I ignored his falter, kind of, and called out, "Hey, there, Little Bear! What brings you out into this neck of the woods?"

"I was, um, in the neighborhood and thought I'd stop in and see how you and Ian were doing," he said as he looked around, as casually as a stunned man could, for signs of my first husband.

"Ian?" Jenny asked. "Why would Daddy's cousin Ian be here?"

I cleared my throat and nudged her with my Judah bearing arm, telling her without words to hush. "oh," she said quietly, taking my hint.

"Oh, you haven't met my family," I said, taking charge of the conversation. "This is Jenny, my adopted daughter, and this is Leo and this is Judah."

"And this is Wren," Jenny added. "And here's a cookie for you. Do you want to come inside for a drink? We have lots of water but I can make you some raspberry leaf tea. It's real good especially if it's got honey in it. We have honey, too. And if you're going to be here for a while, you can eat dinner with us and meet my Daddy and Grandpa Jody and Grannie. And James and Leah are with Poppi, that's my other grandpa, so we'll have more room at the table." Jenny spouted her greeting and plans for the evening like she was practicing to become an auctioneer.

Little Bear grinned at the vivacious girl, thought for a moment, then answered, "Yes, I'd love a cup of tea, that is, if it's not too inconvenient."

Jenny's eyes darted back to me, confused at his words. I nodded, 'yes, go ahead and make the tea,' without spoken words then she darted away, Wren's head bobbing over her shoulder. "Come on in unless you want to unload your mules first," I said. "The men will be back in a bit. I, um, remarried. Ian kind of left me here. Well, hell," I exclaimed as I stopped in the trek to the house and turned to face him, "he dumped me here. I mean, Jody and Sarah were, are, great, and it all turned out fine. I met Jody's son, Wallace, and, well, one thing led to another and he and I wed a few weeks ago when these guys were six-weeks-old."

"These are all yours?" he asked with eyes wide. I nodded yes in answer. "And Ian dumped you?" I nodded again.

Little Bear shook his head in amazement. "It's easier for me to believe you had three beautiful, healthy babies at the same time than to believe that Ian would be so stupid as to leave you—leave you anywhere, even with family."

I shrugged my shoulders; I didn't want to say anything lest it come out mean or angry. I thought I was pretty much over the hurt but having to relate the story had opened up that old wound again. I guess I really didn't need to explain it though. He had met Ian, they had spoken at length, and Little Bear probably knew about Ian's revenge plans long ago.

Little Bear saw my reluctance to speak so changed the subject. "Just after you and, ahem, just after you left last winter, I met your Uncle Jody. Or is he your father-in-law?"

I gave a quick laugh and explained, "He's both my father-in-law and brother-in-law, sort of. You see, Sarah, his wife, is my sister, sort of. We're related but not by blood. It's complicated so we just say we're sisters." There was no way I was going to let him know that Sarah and I were both time travelers born in the 20th century and that my adult daughter and son-in-law were currently visiting his great-great ever so many times over uncle. It wasn't pertinent to anything we would be discussing anyway.

Ж

Little Bear, Jenny, the babies, and I all spent the afternoon in the kitchen. Jenny peeled the potatoes for the stew and baked another batch of cookies as I nursed all the babies and visited. Little Bear regaled us with his lessons on how to trap and skin a beaver and how dangerous they really were even if they looked innocent. An hour later, Jody and Sarah came back from town with as many goodies as they were able to barter for, followed by Wallace, back for the day from his wood cutting project.

"Weel, if it isna my messenger. How are ye, Little Bear?" Jody asked as he shared a hearty handshake. "Oh, Evie, I never did tell ye. I, um, met Little Bear jest before I met ye fer the first time. He told me about ye, that ye were with child. Although I dinna think that he ken ye were havin' three at the same time."

"No, definitely not," Little Bear agreed with a smile.

There was an awkward moment there when no one spoke. It was obvious to me that we had all started thinking about that time nearly a year ago. If that's when Jody had met Little Bear, then he knew that Ian and I had been with him only hours before. Shoot, there was probably more to that story and that's why the men were suddenly tongue-tied. It would be better to ignore the subject than inquire about it. "So, have you got your trapping territory picked out yet? Or do you go back to the same place every year?" I asked, effectively changing the topic and mood of the conversation.

"Oh, I have a new area this year. I just decided to drop in and visit before I got too busy. I didn't know that you'd be here but was pretty sure Jody would know where you were."

"And you wanted to see her baby, huh?" Jenny popped in. "Only you thought there'd only be one. Boy, were you surprised!"

Wallace shot her a look, 'Be respectful, and don't make fun of someone's shock.' Jenny sucked in her lips in embarrassment. Wallace saw that she felt bad; that hadn't been his intent, so he opened up his arms to her, allowing her the opportunity to crawl into his lap. "Yes, I'll bet you were surprised to see Evie with four children and a new husband. But, we're all doing fine. You're welcome to stay as long as you'd like. I'm sure it gets cold and lonely out there."

"Thank you for the offer. I think I'll take you up on it, at least for the night. I'll get a fresh start out in the morning."

Ж

After dinner, Wallace walked with Little Bear to the barn. He could tell the man wanted to ask him something but was hesitant. "Is there something you need or want?" he asked.

"I see you have three milk goats here. I know an Indian family who could really use one. I'd like to trade for one if I could. I, I really don't know what you need though. You seem to have everything a man could want," Little Bear said as he looked around at his surroundings, hoping that his admiration for the man's situation didn't come across as jealousy.

"You're right; I really can't think of anything we need, so how about if I just give her to you? You said you were giving her to another family?"

Little Bear nodded. "Actually more than a family, they're a small tribe. They have several small children and they're just now recovering from a measles epidemic. I'm not sure how much food they have, but a milk goat would really help them out."

"It's a shame that what is just a childhood disease, a minor inconvenience for white people, has caused so many deaths for the Indians. Yes, I'd be more than happy to help them in my small, humble way. Take your pick of the nannies, and if I don't see you before you leave, have a safe trip."

Little Bear shook Wallace's hand wholeheartedly. Evie's husband knew that he would leave early in the morning, before anyone else was awake. Long farewells were uncomfortable for hermits like himself; Wallace must have realized it and had offered his guest the chance to say good-bye the night before departing.

Ж

Little Bear was up and ready for the road when Jenny came running out of the house to see him. It was still dark and he thought everyone would still be asleep. "Would you take these to your friends with the children? There's plenty for you, too. I just thought that they might want some cookies. Is that okay?" Jenny asked hopefully, her eyes blinking back her early morning sleepiness.

"I'm sure they'll all appreciate it. That was very thoughtful of you. Would you say good-bye to your family for me?" he asked, embarrassed that he had been caught leaving without bidding farewell to the generous and compassionate family.

"I will. And, I think I'll be seeing you and your family again, but not for a few years. Be safe," she said, sniffing back the tears. Hopefully, he would think her sadness was just because he was leaving. She couldn't tell him that there would be more unhappiness for his friends before he had a family of his own. But, she could offer him cookies and good wishes to go with the goat that Daddy had given him.

Little Bear put the cookies in his daypack then grabbed the smallest of the milk goats and, as gracefully as he could, climbed onto his mule, balancing the terrified nanny across his lap. He started his journey then turned back and gave Jenny another wave good-bye. One of these days, maybe he'd have a daughter, too.

Jenny waved quickly then ran into the house to her parents and siblings, glad that her Daddy was home—safe and alive.

Asking Evie for her hand in marriage had been a far-fetched possibility. It was just that he had been so taken with her when they met last winter. He couldn't help but hope that she was now available. But, he really was glad she had a good family, a home, a real roof over her head, and even a dress to wear. Wallace seemed like a strong man, a gentle giant like his father, and he definitely cared for their children. Yes, it was time to go back to trapping and forget about a wife and family for a few more years.

Ж

A few hours later

"Well, my little lady, it looks like a little udder relief is needed for you. Let's see if I can still remember how to milk a goat." Little Bear opened up his pack and pulled out his cooking pot. He let the nanny goat walk around, following behind her, holding her little rope leash, until she found a stand of grass that pleased her. He sat down next to her and hummed a tune. "Will Brahms's Lullaby work for you?" he asked. He set the pan on the ground under her and continued his melody. He stroked her hair from her neck down her back, eventually running his hands down her sides then under her belly. He stroked her udder then began milking her. "Just like eating pudding. I guess twenty years doesn't make a difference. Once you've milked a goat, you never forget."

Ж

Little Bear approached the little tribe; they were more of an extended family he realized, and saw the women preparing their evening meal. Or at least Prudence, that is Morning Star, was. Rachel was sitting a few feet away, nursing the little Indian baby. He wasn't trying to sneak up on them, and the men probably already knew he was there and weren't threatened by him, but it was the nanny goat that announced their arrival. All faces turned toward him so he waved, waiting until he was closer to speak.

"Where'd you get the goat?" Morning Star asked.

"My friends, the Pomeroys, gave her to me to give to you. I told Wallace about your, um, dilemma with the measles and he offered her to help feed you."

"I know them!" Rachel crowed. "Did you see Sarah and Evie? How are they? Are the babies getting bigger? How's Jenny?"

"Yes and yes and everyone's fine, and I never saw the babies before, so I wouldn't know if they're bigger, but babies usually keep growing, so I guess they must be bigger."

"Oh, fresh milk will be so nice," Morning Star crooned.

"Oh, and Jenny sent these for you. She baked them herself. They're oatmeal cookies."

"Milk and cookies," Morning Star said as she lifted the parcel to her face and sniffed, "life just keeps getting better and better."

17 The Reluctant Carpenter

The men worked from porritch to potatoes, sunup to sundown, crafting their wood and wattle homes. The days blurred together for Marty. He tried to ignore the time passage, but his internal calendar plagued him like an emotional indigestion, popping in whenever he emptied his mind, churning his stomach and tightening his throat. Two weeks passed by, fifteen days, sixteen, another full moon, the second one since he'd been here; his only relief was the mental numbing of hard work.

Of course, the harder he worked, the more effort the other three men put into the construction effort—they couldn't let a white man, an old white man, outpace them in trimming and notching the timbers. But, the competition was friendly with everyone a winner: the houses were coming together quicker than Red Shirt had figured which meant that the trip to The Trees would be sooner. Marty even constructed an improvised pulley system to hoist the topmost timbers into place. He was humble about the design and even tried to give credit for it to the chief, but Red Shirt wouldn't accept it. Instead, they all took turns employing it, none of them acting as the modern equipment foreman. Each man was able to perform all aspects of the construction and there were no egos involved.

The women had set up their own routine and were comfortable in each other's presence, laughing as they did their chores. "You're the little sister I never had," Morning Star told Rachel.

"Well, you're more than the sister I never had—you're kind of like a mother, too," Rachel replied. She gulped, suddenly afraid that she had insulted her new confidante. "I mean…" she stuttered.

"No, mother is fine. But, big sister is more how I feel with you or think a big sister would feel. I never had any siblings. I didn't have a mother for very long either, so I don't know how to act like one. It's a whole new emotion, the way I feel toward you, Big Sister, and Baby Brother, but it all seems so natural." Morning Star shifted Baby Brother over to her other shoulder and stirred the beans. "I hope instinct kicks in when I have a baby," she added softly, blushing at the words of admission that she had been having sex.

She knew that she had yelled out more than once with her nighttime passion—she had seen the grin on Marty's face when he asked if she was okay the morning after her first time, but she couldn't help it. That first night, their real wedding night, her husband had been so slow and careful. She was the one urging him not to hold back, but he knew what he was doing. The cramping that she felt was less than her monthly, but the pleasure afterwards was more than she thought possible. Sylvester, her fiancé from her old life, had warned her that the first time she had sex, it would hurt, but it would only be that first time. After that, she'd like it as much as he did, he bragged.

She shuddered at the thought of being intimate with that pig of a man. Now she knew how a husband and wife were supposed to be—loving and sharing. No, not just a married couple—a family and tribe, too. Everyone in her immediate family was helpful and supportive. The old women were still distant but weren't as haughty as they had been the first week. At least she didn't have to bear the snorts and prattle that sounded like insults when she walked past their hovel on her way to gather wood. But, that might be because Red Shirt had glowered at them and shook his head when he heard them. If they were rude to her, they'd get less than a child's portion of food that day and a repeat of the head shake and frown at dinner: 'Don't treat my family poorly, or your stomach will suffer.'

Today Big Sister was showing them how to craft pottery by rolling ropes of clay in a circle, building it up then smoothing the surface with a stone. Her work was perfect, but Old Woman and her cane hobbled in and insisted on taking over. The crotchety old crone babbled on in her high, whiny voice, apparently telling Big Sister that she was doing it all wrong. The younger female ceded her coiled bowl to her elder then stepped back to join her new mother and aunt, submissive and respectful of the dowager.

Old Woman set down her bowl of whitish grains and gave her pottery lesson to Big Sister. Rachel and Morning Star didn't have to worry about understanding her words or gestures. She ignored them, so they ignored her. Old Woman carried on with her instructions, adding more wood to the kiln's fire. Apparently, Big Sister needed to be taught the nuances of the firing and curing of pottery.

The pottery finishing instructions continued through most of the day, Rachel and Morning Star wordlessly watching the demonstration in between fixing dinner and tending to babies. Finally, Old Woman called Big Sister over to her, urging her to try her hand at applying the corncob powder to the fiery, nearly red-hot bowl, at last letting her work on her own project. Old Woman put her hands on top of Little Sister's, guiding her in the circular motion needed to sprinkle the matrix over the clay surface. She took two sticks and flipped the bowl, dumping the still smoking corncob ashes out of it, placing the bowl back on top of the smoldering mass to let the smoke cure the inside, thus making the vessel watertight. Old Woman said a few more words then smiled at her pupil, "You did well," she said with her Cherokee words but also with her relaxed body language. She nodded in farewell, adding a couple of words and gestures that the wives could tell meant, "Go ahead and finish by yourself, Big Sister—you know what you're doing."

Then Old Woman did something totally unexpected: she acknowledged Rachel and Morning Star with a smile, then bent over and placed two small bowls at their feet. "These are for us?" Rachel asked innocently.

Old Woman snorted a laugh then swept the back of her hand toward the young wife like she was brushing a fly from her dinner: take them, they're yours.

"Thank you," Morning Star said then glanced at Rachel, telling her with a look: be respectful.

"Oh, thank you, thank you very much," Rachel said obediently then looked back to Morning Star to see if she had done right or should she say more. The mother figure gave a tender grin of acknowledgment to her woman-child sister-daughter: well done.

Old Woman made her way back to her hovel. She hadn't said another word, which was unusual. If it was possible for the crone with the cane to do so, she hobbled with a smile, glad that the men in her family had found hard-working women to help them with their families.

Ж

"I know you said that you needed to build five homes," Marty said to Red Shirt as he signed constructing five units with his hands, "but it looks like four should be enough. I mean, one for you and your family, one for Number Two and his, one for the old women, and then one for The Young One and me—at least for me until I go. I really, really, really want to go home," Marty begged. His voice was pleading and he couldn't help but sink toward the ground. He didn't want to get on his knees, but it seemed that his legs had a mind of their own; they were getting ready to assume the begging position.

"Hmph," Red Shirt snorted then let a little grin escape. He pointed to Dances Naked and gestured for him to stand up; they were going for a walk. Red Shirt pointed to the sky then the ground, to the people working in their little clan then to Marty and himself. He pointed to the sky again and back to the food storehouse.

"Yes, God is good," said Marty. "I think He sent me here for a reason, too. And, I think you know that it's time for me to go. You and your family, your tribe, have everything you need. You have housing and food enough to see you through even the longest winter. You have good people who will work with you, and for you, and even Old Woman has accepted the new wives. Did you know she gave each one of them a bowl? I'm not sure, but I think she means she'll share what's hers with them now. Is that right?"

Red Shirt nodded. His English language skills had been passable, but since Marty had been with them these past two months, it was even better. Of course, speaking with his wife in the evening helped, too. "Home," Red Shirt said to Marty then lifted his chin toward the sunset.

"West, you mean my home, I mean The Trees are to the west?" Marty asked excitedly.

Red Shirt nodded then put up two fingers then looked to the sky. "We can go in two days if the weather stays good?" Marty asked, although he was pretty sure that is what he meant.

Red Shirt nodded then sighed. He really wished the crazy white man would stay with them. He liked him and, although he wasn't as smart as his father, he did care for everyone in the family unit like a grandfather. Yes, the man deserved to be back with his family. If it weren't for him, he wouldn't have food to feed his new wife and son or anyone else.

18 Ready to Rock and Roll

Marty didn't have much to pack but rolling all his worldly possessions together into his bedroll made him feel that much closer to his journey home. He didn't know why Red Shirt wanted to wait two more days, but he'd respect his decision. At least he hadn't stalled or decided that he had to stay to help build that one last building.

He was pretty good at understanding the chief, but it wasn't until later that night, when he was saying his prayers, that he realized the fifth building was to be a church or temple or holy place of some sort. He felt bad, well, a little bit, that he wasn't going to stay and help build it. But, on the other hand, the men now had improved tools to help with the construction and had gained lots of experience building the first four. And, the temple was for members of the tribe—they should be the ones building it, not a crazy white man who did nothing but complain about wanting to be back with his family.

Marty sighed at his self-chastisement. He knew Red Shirt and the others didn't think of him as an outsider. From that first morning when they had found him asleep, an Indian hunting party who had managed to acquire his stolen horse, he liked them. They traded with each other, fed each other, even conspired against a common enemy, Grant, together. But, now the visiting old man was going home.

A sudden panic overtook Marty. Home. Where was it now? Should he stay here with the people he knew? What would happen if James and Leah's ministrations didn't work, and Ian never had another son? What if he died and his son, Scout Kincaid, Bibb's ancestor, was never born? That meant that when, or if, he went back, Bibb wouldn't be there. And, if she wasn't there, then neither Billy nor James would be born…Oh, my God! What would happen to them if their ancestor was never born? Would they just, poof, disappear?

Stop being paranoid, Melbourne! Remember, God has it all under control. It may seem like a great inconvenience, being held back from your family for a couple of months, but look what you've accomplished. Yes, you were able to buy food for the group so they didn't starve over the winter. Rachel would probably be with Red Shirt no matter what. But Prudence, now called Morning Star; if you hadn't been there to intercede, would Old Woman have cast her out, and Red Shirt forced to return her to her father? If that had happened, then Number Two would not have a wife, and Big Sister and Baby Brother would be without a mother—at least not her. No, it's all going to be fine.

Ж

"Rachel, I think I'm pregnant. I'm not too sure about this, but I haven't had my menses since I've been here and that's almost two months, I mean two moons. I mean, well, you know what I mean. You've been pregnant before, isn't that what happens?" Morning Star asked.

"You mean your courses," Rachel asked, "the bleeding?"

Morning Star nodded her head in embarrassment. Her father had given her a book about anatomy to tell her about becoming a woman. Her mother had died when she was three, and her father did the best he could. The book helped, but she only knew the medical terms, not the common name, for the monthly bleeding. She saw other women in church and had gone to school, but nobody ever talked about those things with her.

"Well, I never had any, I mean, I just got pregnant, had a baby, got pregnant again…" Rachel stopped talking when she saw the shocked look on her friend's face. "I had a baby a few weeks before I came to the tribe. She was born dead. I didn't know anything, well, not much, about babies before. But Sarah, she's a nice lady and the healer who helped, um, take care of the birthin', she had a long talk with me. But, you're right. I haven't had one either. I think we're both pregnant. I think we're having twins!"

"Twins?" Morning Star asked in a loud whisper, trying to contain her excitement. "I mean, I'm pretty sure I'm pregnant, but you're pregnant, too?"

Rachel nodded excitedly, holding back the urge to jump up and down and squeal.

Morning Star calmed down before speaking again. "I think we're going to have two babies, but they won't be twins," the elder lady-in-waiting explained. "You have to have two babies come out of the same womb to be twins. But, two babies! Have you told Red Shirt yet?"

Rachel shook her head. "No, but I think he knows. I mean, he's been looking at the moon every night then down at me, grinning real big like, just before, um, we, you know…"

Rachel's voice trailed off; Morning Star knew what she meant. Her husband did the same thing. The men knew they had more members of the tribe coming and were proud of it.

Ж

Marty made sure he stayed busy all day. He was probably overtaxing himself, but he had so much nervous energy, it was either work twice as hard as usual or drive himself crazy by looking up at the sky every five minutes, wishing for the day to be over so it would be night, then morning, then he and Red Shirt could leave for The Trees.

When Marty and the others came in for a drink and a light lunch, he could tell something was different. Red Shirt brought out the ham, carved off a hearty portion of it, then handed it to Morning Star to cook.

The chief knew he should probably offer his wife the honor but also knew that Morning Star was the better cook; he didn't want the meat spoiled or overcooked. He handed his wife the largest cabbage and ten potatoes. She had made soup and baked potatoes before and he knew she could do it again. Tonight they were going to have a celebration.

Ж

The smell of baked ham pulled the men from the woods, their lumber harvesting done for the day. And, done for a lifetime, too, his lifetime anyway, Marty realized.

The area around the cooking fire looked extra clean. Marty saw Big Sister with her grass broom, sweeping the silty dirt and rocks into a swirling pattern. She looked up and smiled at him then bent back to her task. She wanted tonight to be perfect for Dances Naked, the man who her uncle had once said was of great use to them. Tonight he would become much more than that—he would officially become a member of their family.

The wives came out from their homes, carrying their babies and the eating bowls. Old Woman came from her new residence, leading her little coterie of crones to the common eating area, her familiar gnarled wood staff replaced by her ceremonial crook, the one decorated with wood-burned characters and topped with feathers. She stood as tall as she could, her usual snarl replaced by a gapped-tooth smile. It had been too long since they had dressed up for a celebration or had a reason for one. Her grandson wouldn't tell her the purpose of the event, but she knew the time was near for Dances Naked to go home. She didn't think her grandson was happy to see him leave, he might even be sad about it, but he was man enough to honor the crazy white man who had found a way to help feed and house them. Dances Naked wasn't as good-looking as her husband had been, but he was a good provider and nice to her great-grandchildren. She'd be happy to honor him, too.

Red Shirt motioned for everyone to gather for dinner. It was time for his announcements. His words were short and his gestures easy for the white women and Marty to understand. Red

Shirt placed his fist over his heart then over Marty's, 'You are part of me, my family,' he said wordlessly.

"Thank you, and thanks for the hospitality," Marty said. "And, if I didn't have my other family to go back to, I'd stay with you forever." He nodded in appreciation, sniffing back the tears that he was sure the Cherokee would see as a sign of weakness. Even if he was leaving in the morning, he didn't want to be remembered as a lesser man.

The old women started to sit down but were stopped by a grunt from Red Shirt: he had more to say. He called Number Two to his side with a gesture and a grin. Number Two brought his wife with him and stood next to his chief, proud to be of service to the brave man who always inspired hope. Next, Red Shirt grunted to Rachel then pointed to Big Sister, indicating that he wanted her to give their son to the girl to watch.

Rachel wasn't sure what he meant, but Morning Star knew that the two wives were part of the ceremony, and the children weren't needed, at least for this part. "Give Big Sister your son," she whispered.

"Oh," Rachel said then handed him to the young girl who was already holding Baby Brother. She really wished the Indians talked more. She had a hard time trying to figure out what her husband wanted unless he told her with words.

Red Shirt looked to Number Two and flipped his head back: let's tell them. At the same time, the two men placed their right hands over their wives wombs and smiled. The tribe was going to grow, there were two more members to be born in less than a year.

Ж

Everyone enjoyed the perfect meal then went to bed early. The extra full bellies made them tired, plus Red Shirt and Marty were going to leave at sunrise. The white man was finally going home.

171

Red Shirt didn't want to go all the way to The Trees but knew that Dances Naked had no sense of direction. He had seen him get lost, or nearly so, just coming back from getting wood. But, maybe this time would be different. He was going to his family. The urgency of it was sure to make a difference to him.

Ж

Marty couldn't sleep. He felt like he had just downed two pots of coffee but knew it was only the excitement of being so close to home. He lay flat on his back, wishing he had another blanket. The Young One was hot blooded and probably would rather he didn't have any fire at all until winter, but they compromised and the fire was kept low.

Marty made sure The Young One was asleep then pulled out the little laminated photograph that James had given him before they parted ways two months ago. He leaned close to the fire and tried to see the faces in the picture. The glow was too dim, but it didn't matter; he had memorized every detail and nuance down to the number of flowers on the hospital gown Bibb was wearing. He rubbed the inside right seam of his vest and felt it—the ancient Greek coin. He'd need that, too, for his trip through The Trees.

Ж

Just before sunrise, Red Shirt came into the single men's house and found him. Marty had finally fallen asleep, his face on the rock next to the dying coals, the photograph of his family lying face up in his open hand. Red Shirt held his fiery torch near it, curious about what it was. He squatted down and took a close look at the shiny object. He pulled his neck back, unwilling to believe that Dances Naked had people captured in that flat piece of still water. He touched it with his finger, making sure it wasn't ice that was holding in the little spirits, fairies that entered a man's dreams at night and told him secrets.

Marty woke up to the smell of fire. He looked up and saw Red Shirt staring at him then back at the photo he had in his hand. What could he do? "These are my family," he said.

Red Shirt gasped in horror: the crazy white man had his family trapped in warm ice.

"No, not my family. I mean, yes, they're my family, but this is only a photograph, a representation, of them. See, that's my, um, wife, Bibb. She had just been beat up, that is hit, by some very bad men. This is my youngest son, James. He's the one who is staying with the Pomeroys now. And, this is Billy. I never knew he had even been born until recently. His mother, well, I just found out about him. He was, how should I say, hidden from me." Marty looked up and saw he wasn't getting anywhere with his explanation. It was too much for Red Shirt to comprehend, at least the technology of capturing a person's essence in a photograph.

"This is what my family looks like; these are not their spirits in here. I want to go home now, okay?"

Red Shirt sighed in relief. He didn't think that Dances Naked was a soul stealer. He had seen paintings in the city two years ago, but this one was smaller and of much better quality. It must be that where his friend lived, on the other side of The Trees, they had smaller paintbrushes and better artists.

"Can we go now," Marty asked. He put his picture back in the inside pocket of his vest. He didn't mean for anyone to see it but was glad that Red Shirt was only mildly taken aback. There was a lot of trust between them. He had never had a brother, but now he did. And, now he was leaving another member of his family. But, Bibb and Billy needed him. And, he needed them.

Red Shirt led the way out of the house and away from their town, never looking back. But, Marty wasn't returning. He wanted one last look at the little community he had helped construct. It was early and everyone was asleep. Or so he thought. Morning Star came out of her house, Baby Brother over her shoulder.

Evidently, he had awakened early and a cup of milk wouldn't work for him: he wanted his Nanny Rachel.

Morning Star was an Indian by choice but a white woman by birth. She couldn't hold back the emotions like the red man. "Oh, Marty, we're going to miss you. I owe you everything. I mean, if it weren't for you, Old Woman would have sent me on my way that first night. If it's okay with my husband, I'd like to name our first child after you, at least his middle name."

Marty chuckled. "And, if you have a daughter, the middle name of Martina would be quite flattering. I'm sure you'll make a good mother for your first born because you're already doing so well with your first two." Marty gave her a big-brotherly hug then stuffed his little bedroll back under his arm. "Let's go," he said to Red Shirt, once again trying to hide those sneaky tears that kept popping out.

Ж

The two men rode all day in silence. It was Red Shirt's nature to be quiet, but Marty, normally chatty even if it was only a one-sided conversation, was absorbed in his own fantasies, hopes, and fears, so overwhelmed by the magnitude of his thoughts, that he couldn't find the confidence to speak.

"There," Red Shirt said aloud, his deep voice startling Marty, bringing him out of his reverie.

"Right through there?" Marty asked, still stunned by hearing his red brother speak.

Red Shirt frowned at him: don't make me speak again. But, the crazy white man's obvious fear and uncertainty overrode Red Shirt's personal indignation about verbalizing. "When you wake in the morning, walk away from the sunrise."

"Go west?" Marty asked as he pointed to the sunset, "and you'll take the mare back with you?"

Red Shirt nodded but said no more. He had given simple directions that even a child could follow.

"Why didn't you speak before?" Marty asked.

Red Shirt shrugged his shoulders. He didn't want to tell him that he only had so many words to share, and he wanted to save them in case his new brother changed his mind and decided to return to live with him and his tribe instead of going through the Bad Medicine Trees. He cared for the man both like a brother and an uncle, and hoped he would stay, but it was doubtful he could be swayed. Deep down, he knew Dances Naked would spend his last breath, if necessary, trying to get back to his family. He knew he would, too, if their places were switched. It had only been two days since they left their home, but he already missed his family more than he thought possible. He even missed his ornery old grandmother.

Ж

Red Shirt arose just before daylight, leaving Dances Naked asleep near the fire, the smile on the old man's face showing he was at peace with his decision to go home. The Indian chief pulled out a parting gift for his new brother, a thick slab of ham for breakfast. If it hadn't been for the white man's shrewd bartering, he wouldn't have it to share. He didn't want to wake him, so left the meat wrapped in the cotton fabric, torn from his sister-in-law's former petticoat, providing a scent barrier to the sweet, salty smell of the cured pork. He got on his horse and rode away, atop the mare that was the first gift Dances Naked had given him. He scratched his balls, the coarseness of the cotton cloth of his pants, Dances Naked's second gift to him, still an irritant at times to his man parts. The man was generous, faithful, and funny. He sure hoped his wife and child cared for him as much as his other family, his Indian family, did.

Ж

Marty awoke to the smell of ham. At first, he thought it was a dream, and then he saw it. Flies were attracted to the faint smell and were landing on the white, cotton covered parcel two feet away, trying to extract sustenance from it. "Get away from that," Marty said as he shooed his hand over the package, "that's my breakfast!"

He looked up and saw he was alone. The sun was just peeking over the horizon; that way was east. Red Shirt had told him he was to travel away from the sunrise. "I'm on my way, family," he crowed, startling the birds that had gathered in the nearby bushes. "I'll stop for breakfast later."

Marty set a quick pace. The clouds were coming in and he knew he was directionally challenged. He spotted a clump of trees off in the distance then traveled to it. He repeated the process until his rumbling tummy and weak knees told him that it was time to eat. "Good enough spot for an early lunch," he commented to the spreading tree. He kicked away the larger stones and used the side of his well-worn boot to smooth a seat for himself. "Not this time," he said as he drew a long arrow in the dusty soil, indicating the direction he was to travel when he was done with his meal.

The slice of ham Red Shirt had given him was generous and enough for two meals at least. The only problem was that the salty repast made him thirsty. He still had water in his canteen but didn't know where there was a creek nearby. His Indian friends knew where all the little springs were in this area, but he didn't. Certainly, there was a trick to finding them, or maybe it was just that they were that familiar with the territory. "Just a little sip, and then I'll save the rest for later," he told himself, then toped half a mouthful. He carefully rewrapped the remaining meat, placed it inside his bedroll, then got up to continue his journey home, glad that he had remembered to etch his directional marker in the soil before brunch.

Marty fought back the urge to sprint to his next reference point, realizing that, even though it was at least late October, he was likely to become overheated with the extra exertion. Instead, he paced himself, marching out at a brisk walking pace rather than a slow jog. "Better the tortoise than the hare," he remarked aloud, remembering that sure and steady wins the race.

"Who goes there?" hollered a gruff voice just ahead of him.

"*C'est moi!*" Marty bragged. "It's me, myself and I. We're just passing through and will be gone as fast as these old man legs can take us."

"Well, good," the man behind the bushes said. "Let me lighten your load a little then, so you can get out of here even faster," he added sarcastically and walked out to present himself.

Grant was back.

Marty gulped hard and managed to stay on both feet although his knees didn't think it was such a great idea. Grant had a knife: a rougher, cruder version than his previous bone-handled one. This one had rags tied around the hilt, but it still had a blade. The cocky bandit was wielding it like it was a Samurai sword, slicing the air with his broad motions, pretending his little eight inch blade was a full forty inches long. "Well, what do you have for me, mister?" he barked when his air dueling exhibition was over.

Marty stayed mum but tossed his bedroll over to the mangy man's feet. It appeared Grant didn't remember him, and he wasn't going to remind him that he was the one who had helped bury him two months ago. Evidently, he had managed to dig himself out of his Cherokee tomb with the little shard of wood he had left with him. Or, some idiot came along and dug him out. Either way, Marty was in harm's way with the shiftless highwayman, the man with no morals who used to torment and beat his sister, Rachel, for fun.

Rachel. Suddenly Marty remembered Rachel and her new family. Surely, there was no way Grant would find his way back to her. He sent up a silent prayer, 'keep them safe,' then realized Rachel had a husband, an entire under-populated tribe, to protect her, and keep her and her young son safe. Marty's eyes went skyward, 'A little help here, too, Lord,' he prayed silently, hoping again that Grant would not remember him and would leave him with at least his life, and maybe his water, too.

Marty had subconsciously looked at his canteen, half-hidden under his vest, as he said his prayer. Grant saw the eye movement and pointed to the water can. "I'll relieve you of that, too. I wouldn't want to slow you down with such a heavy load," he said, ending his pitiful joke with an evil laugh.

Marty started to protest but thought his chances of surviving a daylong trek without water were better than a minute-long confrontation with a mad man and his knife. He leaned his head forward and took his neck and shoulders out from under the canteen's strap, biting down on the words, 'Take it and get out of here,' before they got up to his throat. He didn't say them but thought them hard enough, making sure that he kept his scowling face low so Grant didn't get a good look at him.

"You know, I'd kill you just for practice..." Grant stated, and then waited for his prey to look up at him and beg.

But, Marty wasn't buying into it. He had always been a proud man, too proud by many people's standards, but he had learned from his Cherokee friends not to grovel, that you took what life had to offer and made do with it without demeaning yourself. He wasn't going to look up, but realized that by ignoring Grant, he was probably irritating him even more. Instead, he played a third role: the sick man. He fell to his knees and started coughing, hoping that he'd start gagging and maybe even bring up a bit of his late breakfast. Vomit had a way of turning away everyone's head. Surely, Grant wouldn't attack a sick man, or chance getting puked on.

Marty's ploy worked. "Ah, I hope you choke to death," Grant said, then walked over to the bushes from whence he came. He grabbed the reins of a swaybacked nag and led her a few yards away to a low spot in the terrain. He stood beside her, clutched her mane, and jumped up, managing to get onto her back in an almost comedic fashion, legs kicking, and belly squirming against the mare's spine, his awkwardness as amazing as the fact that he had completed the feat. Marty bit his bottom lip to keep from laughing then remembered to start coughing and dry heaving again. Hopefully, the idiot on the bareback horse would be gone before he needed to produce any regurgitated food.

And then he was gone, out of sight and sound, almost as quickly as he had appeared, riding into the east, not a care in the world as he took a pull from the canteen he had taken from Marty. "Shit, just water," he carped as he dumped out the clear fluid. "I gotta find me some whisky."

Ж

Marty turned to the left, turned to the right, then pivoted around twice. "Shit," he said as he wiped the slobber from the sides of his mouth. He had managed to keep his food in but had made a mess out of his beard with the feigned vomit—the spittle evidently was enough to repulse Grant. "Which way did he go?" Marty had lost track of his own direction and even the knowledge that Grant had been heading the opposite direction of him was of no use to him now; he couldn't see or remember which direction the fiend had left.

19 After the Trees
Late October, 1782 and 2013

'Wow! There they are. I'll bet I walked right past them two, maybe three times. I didn't think about the leaves changing colors,' Marty thought. He smacked his lips, trying to work up at least enough moisture to swallow. His little trick didn't work this time but only encouraged a cough.

Marty leaned over and placed his hands on his bare knees, concentrating on a smooth, slow air intake, trying to stifle his cough. 'You're a yogi, you're a yogi,' became his silent mantra. 'You can control your breath—slow in, slow out. You're a yogi, hold the breath; exhale.'

He knew his mind was going kaput. He wasn't crazy but physiologically, he was shutting down. He had gone too many days without food and only had a few drops of dew to drink in the last three days. The grass he ate had tasted great, but the diarrhea he suffered from eating too much at once and in its raw state had debilitated his body even further. His problem had a name: electrolyte imbalance. He knew what it was and how to cure it but didn't have the raw materials on hand. Good old sugar and salt mixed in water, an off the shelf sports drink, would fix him right up. He also knew the results of not getting the sweetened saline solution either orally or intravenously: cardio shutdown. His heart would stop beating. He could already tell it was thump, thump, thudding erratically. 'You're a yogi, you can control everything; you're a yogi, you can control your heart beats...'

He wanted to lie down and rest. "nope," he mumbled aloud, as if verbalizing his conviction would hold sway over his weakened body and mind. They were both at the end of their usefulness, but his determination was still at 100%. He raised his hands in prayer, "Lord, please just get me back to my family so they can take care of the rest of me. You got my attention. It's You, not some yogi, who's in charge of my heart, lungs, and everything else."

Marty lowered his arms and placed his right hand over his shirt pocket, pulling out the laminated picture of his sons, James and Billy, and their mother, his purple-faced but glowing with pride Bibb, still recovering from her bashing by the MacLeod brothers. "I'm coming, I'm coming," he whispered coarsely then looked at the time portal. This time he was sure that these were the right trees. He clutched his empty belly and felt the queasiness that confirmed the site. He tilted his head up, and croaked, "Thanks," to the Lord, and walked straight up to the timber gateway, clutching his ancient Greek drachma, his silver ticket. "mysterious ways," he mumbled as he briefly recalled the strange events of the last few months. "mysterious ways,' he repeated softly, then strode through the two sentinels, his vision of Bibb held in his mind as tight as he held his ancient coin in his trembling hand. "I'm coming home."

Ж

"Good Lord, who, what's that?" screeched the lady realtor in the tacky, gray jogging suit. "Eww! It's moving!"

Mrs. Goodwin scurried backwards away from the unconscious, wild-haired old man clad solely in a ratty, torn shirt. She looked down, noticed his limited wardrobe, and hissed, "He doesn't have on any pants!" She turned and dashed the five yards to her shiny blue SUV, broke a fingernail pulling at the latch, cursed mildly, jumped into the driver's seat, locked the doors, started the engine, and peeled out from the vacant lot, flinging back dirt and gravel over the prone figure. Her left, white knuckled hand grasped the steering wheel as she blindly rummaged through her little crocheted handbag with her right, finally locating her cell phone. She pressed and held the numeral nine with her thumb, speed dialing the Greensboro Police Department before she was even a hundred yards away.

"911—what's your emergency?" the operator asked.

"There, there's a, a thing out there at the old Robbins' place. I think it wanted to kill me!" Cindy babbled hysterically. "It was horrible!"

"Ma'am, are you hurt?"

"No, no; I got away. I, I'm sorry. I guess I shouldn't have called. It's just that I thought that he was going to hurt me," she apologized.

"Ms. Goodwin?" the operator asked.

"Um, yes," Cindy replied, "this is her."

"Ms. Goodwin, you have to stop calling us every time you think that there's someone out to get you. You've cried wolf so many times that if there really was an emergency, well, we'd still respond to it, but you're causing undue stress on our limited resources."

Cindy gulped in embarrassment then uttered a heartfelt, "Sorry."

"Now, if there isn't anyone hurt or in immediate danger, I'll go ahead and hang up," Dyane said. This wasn't her usual job; she was the vacation replacement for the regular dispatcher, but she knew all about Cindy and her panic calls.

"Wait, wait," Cindy blurted out, desperately trying to save face. "There is someone out there. I mean, he probably wasn't going to hurt me, but he was on the ground and not moving and, really, maybe you ought to send someone out there. He's right under the big for sale sign, just before you get to the old Robbins' place."

"Okay, Ms. Goodwin, I'll get an officer out there right away. Thank you and good-bye," Dyane said, then disconnected the call.

"If you don't need me for anything, Dyane, I'm going home," Billy said as he popped his head in the dispatch office. His shift was over and he had a big bed with his name on it, just waiting for him to plop down and get some much needed shut eye. It had been a long night.

"There's nothing but another 'Cindy call.' She said there's an old man passed out, there by the old Robbins' place. You know, where that woman and crazy old man disappeared a few months ago? I'll just send a patrol car out there. You know her," Dyane said with an eye roll and finger twirl around her ear, indicating the woman was cuckoo.

Billy inhaled sharply. "Uh, no; don't bother," he said. "I'll just take a drive out there on my way home. There won't be any overtime involved: I'll give this one to the city," he said with a fabricated smile. "See you tonight," he added, giving her a salute in farewell.

Billy walked out of the building, his phony smile still locked in place. "Just a few more yards to the truck," he said softly through clenched teeth and taut lips. He opened the door of 'The Beast,' his red '64 Dodge pickup truck, buckled up, powered up, and backed out of his parking spot, nearly bumping into a slow moving pedestrian.

"Watch where you're going, asshole!" screamed the bleached blond, middle-aged barfly, punctuating her remark with a middle-fingered gesture and glare.

"Sorry," he said, then double-checked to make sure he wasn't endangering any other inmate's friends or relatives on their way to the jail for visiting hours.

As soon as he was out of the parking lot and onto the highway and its blessed anonymity, he let his face relax. Could it be that his father had come back? The site that Dyane had referred to was where he had picked up this same truck after his brother, James, and best friend in the whole world, Leah, went back in time to the 18th century. It was also where Leah's mother had disappeared a few weeks before that, her destination that same, 232 years in the past, time period.

Billy shook his head. It was too much to hope for. It was his business philosophy to keep an open mind when approaching the scene of a crime. Or an incident, he reminded himself. Hopefully, the old man Cry Wolf Cindy had reportedly seen was really only passed out, not dead.

Billy slowed down as he approached The Trees, watching his route carefully to be sure he didn't run into or over someone. He left the road and took the often used, but unpaved, shortcut to the Robbins' place.

And there he was.

Billy stopped the truck, took two quick, sharp breaths, then pushed open his door and immediately puked on the ground. He turned his head, wiped his mouth on his sleeve, and held onto the side of the truck, hugging the flanks of the steel behemoth for both physical and emotional support. First, his stomach had failed him, and now his knees had forgotten how to keep his thighs and shins in alignment. He clutched the top of the truck's bed, pulled himself up straight, and turned back to look at the person on the ground again. Yes, he was breathing, or at least moving his hand toward his head. Dead men don't move.

Billy didn't remember running to his father's side. He was just there as soon as he saw that he was alive.

"Dad?" he asked hopefully.

Marty forced open one eye and whispered, "Billy?" then shut his eye again and smiled. "Water, please," he mouthed then let his relieved smile take over his face. He was home.

Billy sprinted back to the truck and brought his plastic water bottle with him. He held up his father's head, and dribbled a few drops at a time into his mouth. "Just a little bit to start with, okay?"

Marty sniffed then nodded that he understood. He felt like he was crying. Emotionally he was—the tight throat, urge to sniff, and chest heaves were all there, but his body was so dried up that it couldn't produce a tear. He was home and his son, the son he never knew he had, was taking care of him.

"Dad, I'm going to take you to the hospital. Now, I'm not a doctor, but I have had quite a bit of first aid training, and it looks to me like you're severely dehydrated. I don't want to wait for an ambulance, so you just let me carry you, okay?"

Marty answered by tightly squeezing his eyes, sending up a silent prayer that he would make it to the hospital. His heart's thump, thump, thudding was now thump, thud, thudding; his ticker wasn't beating right.

Billy assessed the situation before acting. Where should he put him? Should he be seated in the front so he could keep an eye on him or should he lay the frail man in the bed of the truck where there would be less stress on his body? The hospital was nearly a half hour away. No, twenty minutes, maybe less: he had the magnetic mount siren behind the seat. He could make a path through traffic and still beat the time of any ambulance dispatched to retrieve him. But, he didn't have an IV bag of Ringer's lactate solution or an EMT standing by to administer it. Marty was in rough shape. He needed to get to the hospital ASAP and a prone position would probably be easier on his severely dehydrated body.

Billy opened out the tailgate of the truck and threw in his jacket. He'd arrange it as a pillow later. "Here, have a little bitty bit more water before you get in the back." He dribbled a few more drops into the parted cracked lips. "Okay, how's your stomach? You're not going to puke, are you?"

Marty's eyes were still shut. It hurt to open them and he knew why. They were totally dried out. There wasn't any lubricating moisture left between his desiccated orbs and the papery sheaths that served as eyelids. He shook his head in answer to Billy's question. He was going to will that bit of moisture to stay inside him. Besides, the water he had already

185

drunk never made it to his stomach. It had been absorbed by the lining of his mouth, his tongue, and his parched gullet. He couldn't open his eyes to get another look at his son, but he could smile at him. Hopefully, they would have time to talk and gaze at each other later. He could only pray that he would pull through, so he did.

Billy gently pulled Marty up into a seated position, wrapped the old man's arm around his neck, grasping him around his bony back with one arm, the other under the knees. "On three," he said, and then lifted him from his squatted position to a wide stance, grunting just a little on his way up. His father was definitely lean but still a tall man and not scrawny. He steadied himself and his load then asked, "Ready to go?"

Marty replied with a gentle squeeze of his arm around Billy's shoulder. The excited son loaded with his feeble father shuffled to the truck. "I'm going to set you in. Hold on," he commanded as he shifted his father's weight, lifting him onto the tailgate. "Now don't go falling out," he ordered as he let go so he could jump in and settle him into the bed.

"Here, use this as a pillow, and then..." Billy said as he wadded up his windbreaker under the old man's head. He pulled a red bandana out of his front pocket and shook it out, "I'll put together a fluid delivery system."

Billy jumped out of the truck and ran back to retrieve the water bottle. He looked around quickly to see if there was anything he had missed; his detective nature was still functional and on high alert. "Yup," he said as he picked up the small silver coin in the dirt and stuck it in his pocket, "we don't want to leave you here."

Billy jumped into the back of the pickup. "I don't want you drinking, but I think this will work to keep your mouth moist. Here, I wet my bandana and then stuck one end in the water bottle. Don't let the bottle fall over," Billy said as he stuffed it among the creases of the jacket, "but go ahead and take a pull every once in a while. Can you handle that?"

Marty nodded, his eyes still closed and the smile of serenity still pasted on his tanned, leathery face. He couldn't talk but did sigh deeply, letting his son know he was ready to hit the road to the hospital.

"Gotcha," Billy said joyfully as he realized he could understand the tacit communication. "I'm not going to spare the rubber, but I won't be taking any fast corners either, so you won't be rolling around back here. I'll see you at the hospital, Dad." He smiled at the designation then bent down and kissed his father on the forehead, hoping he hadn't lingered too long with the buss he thought he would never be able to give.

Billy called for support from his cell phone as soon as he hit the main highway. Two squad cars with sirens and lights joined his blue light, horn honking, fast-paced procession to the hospital. His escorts made sure he made it through the construction zone without delay. The truck drivers didn't like that they had to wait, but then again, they only had a road to pave and not a man on the verge of death who needed medical attention.

The hospital's emergency room nurses, a gurney, and IV delivery system were ready and waiting behind the double doors before the truck was in sight. The truck pulled to a stop and two hefty interns were right there to lift Marty onto the gurney. They paused after letting the tailgate down. They could see that Billy wanted to be the one to move him to the end of the truck. "We're here, Dad," he said, gently pulling the red handkerchief away from the frail man's mouth. "These guys and gals will put you back together again in no time. And, I made a quick call to Mom. She'll be here soon."

Marty's eyes popped open. Evidently, he had enough fluid in him to allow his eyelids to work again. "Yes, Bibb's on her way," Billy said gently. "I'll bring her in as soon as she gets here. Thanks for coming home."

Billy followed behind the nurses and intern a little too closely. "Billy, now you know we know what we're doing here. Why don't you wait out in the lobby? We'll let you know what's going on," the big, dark-skinned male intern suggested strongly.

"Not this time, Nate; he's my father, and you'll need more muscle power than you have to pull me away," Billy said with a judicious mix of mirth and determination. He knew Nate had been a wide receiver for the Carolina Panthers, was twice his size, and probably three times as strong as he was, but he'd waited too long to be with his father to be sent out to wait in some holding pattern.

"Okay, I'll make an exception this time, you bein' a cop and all. But, if you start to get squeamish, I'd appreciate it if you found a place away from us to lose your cookies."

"No worries," Billy said as he smacked the big button on the wall to get inside the emergency room's doublewide doors. "You won't even know I'm here."

The first order of business was to start an IV. The overhead lights were as bright as the sunny morning outside, but that didn't help the big man get the cannula inserted. "shit," Nate mumbled.

"What's wrong?" Billy whispered loudly. "Is he okay? Do you need a hand? Can I help?"

Nate exhaled loudly in frustration. "Yes, you can. You can go out into the lobby and drink about three quarts of water. Your dad is so dehydrated that I'm having a hell of a time finding a vein. I'll get a smaller gauge, but you really need to be out of here—you're getting on my nerves."

"Come on, Billy," Nurse Mandy said as she put her hand on Billy's elbow. "It probably won't rehydrate your father when you drink for him but, hey, it's worth a try. Besides, I think he'll be able to relax more if you aren't so close. You have a tremendous amount of negative energy bouncing all over the place. Remember what Leah always said, 'Negative energy keeps away the healing,' or something like that."

"Okay, I'll go. Hey, Dad," Billy called back, "I'm going to drink a gallon of water for you. Don't let him hurt you or I'll kick his butt!"

Marty managed to open one eye. He looked up and saw the size of the doctor-type person. He looked like an armored truck on steroids. "You'd better do like he said," he whispered to Nate then chortled softly. "And, don't worry about hurting me; just get it done."

Nate grabbed a smaller gauged cannula and got the line started. "Sorry for the extra pokes there, sir. This solution will have you feeling better in no time. Now, while we're waiting, I want you to have some sips of this," Nate offered him the straw and the orange flavored medical grade sports drink, "and then I'm going to give you a bit of a sponge bath. Unless you'd rather have Nurse Mandy do that for you."

Marty shook his head minimally; he still had a monster headache from the dehydration. He swallowed and realized he had some spit in his mouth now and could probably speak in a normal voice. "Ahem, Lord, thank you for the saliva, and good hospital help, and, well, everything. No, if you don't want to do it, go ahead and send my son in here. We have a lot of catching up to do and I'm sure he can talk and scrub at the same time."

"Did you call?" Billy asked as he poked his head into the room, his smile brighter than the high intensity spotlight above the examining table.

"Here," Nate said as he handed Billy the empty plastic tub. Fill 'er up at the sink and then you can make use of this." Nate waved the plastic wrapped sponge at him. "I'll go grab some washcloths and hand towels. Wet 'em, then spread them on the thin skinned areas of his body, like his wrists and neck. You'd be surprised how much moisture skin will absorb topically."

"You're just being kind about the stink, Doc," Marty said. "It's been a long time since I've enjoyed a bath or a shower, and I guess if you can't scrub me up fast enough, then you can go ahead and cover me up with wet towels." Marty pulled the light blanket off his thigh with his non-punctured left hand and stuck his foot out. "I think we're going to have to throw these boots away. I pretty much wore them out."

"Um, what happened to your pants or do I want to know?" Nate asked.

"It's a long story," Billy interjected, "and we'll tell you all about it, more or less, at Dad's homecoming party. I'll make sure you get an invitation. In the meantime, let me get him cleaned up. And, if you see a very beautiful gray-haired lady out there in the waiting room looking a bit anxious, that's probably my mother. Could you escort her in? I'm sure Dad wants to see her right away, pants or no."

"Sure, but, um, I thought you were an orphan like me," Nate said softly, hoping the old man didn't hear him.

"That's another long story and, as you can see, it has a happy ending. How long does he need to stay here?" Billy asked.

"Well, we'll let him get juiced up with the Ringers lactate, and then do a blood test to make sure all his levels are good, and then he should be ready to rock and roll. That is, unless he has other problems he didn't mention." Nate spoke loudly directly to Marty, "You didn't break an arm or a leg and forget to tell us about it, did you?"

"Nope," Marty said as he grabbed his drink and took another sip. "One arm working fine, the other only restricted by the plumbing you stuck in me. Now, how about that bath, son?"

Nate nodded and exited without saying a word. Billy was a good man and was one reason he was able to go back to medical school. A good detective was worth more than his weight in gold. In his case, Billy's diligence had kept him free, out of prison or worse, after the extortion accusations had been proved false.

James Bradford had skipped bail before coming to court, but Nate's good name had been cleared.

Ж

"Oh, Dad, it looks like I have some help here. Or would you rather give him the bath all by yourself, Mom?" Billy asked cheerfully.

Marty looked up and saw Bibb, the mother of his two sons, standing arm in arm with Nate.

"Oh, um, I mean…" Marty stammered. He brought his left hand up to cover his face, hiding his eyes and mouth, as he tried to compose himself. He had planned what he was going to say to her for the last two months, and now all of the sudden, he was as tongue-tied as a four-year-old sitting on Santa's lap.

"How are you feeling?" Bibb asked, not sure what else to say. She had hoped he'd come back from the 18th century, but never allowed herself to believe he really would, so never thought about what to say if he did return.

Marty dropped his hand to his lap and asked, "Will you marry me? I mean, I'd like to get down on one knee or both knees or hell, after what I've put you through the last thirty years, I should be down on my belly, at least, begging you to forgive me, and well, will you, marry me, that is?"

Marty finally found the nerve to look her directly in the eyes. He saw the shocked look on her face and his fear turned into joy. She hadn't expected his question. "Well, will you?" he asked again, this time with confidence that she'd say yes.

"Just try and stop me. I mean, you're not going to change your mind are you? I mean, you're not hallucinating, or in shock, or going to forget all about this as soon as you're feeling better, are you?"

Bibb's stammering only increased Marty's ardor. "Are you sure I can't go home yet?" Marty asked Nate half in jest.

Nate cocked his head and tried to find a way to tell him he'd have to wait another hour, at least. Billy interrupted and saved him the deed. "I know a preacher who does hospital weddings. All you need is a license and you're ready to say your I do's. James and Leah were married right down the hall."

"Or, I can get better and we can go to the British Embassy in Charlotte. It's a couple of hours away, but I think I can pull a few strings and maybe get a proxy wedding set up, me being a subject of the Crown, and you being a Yankee and all," Marty drolled in his attempt at a southern accent.

Bibb was shocked at his suggestion. It was obvious he had thought about this for quite a while and it wasn't a stress-induced fantasy. Marty saw she was speechless and added, "Unless you want to wait and have a big wedding with doves and ice sculptures and acres and acres of roses…"

"Uh, no; just a little affair with you and Billy and, um, one or two others, will be fine with me. I just want you to get your strength back," Bibb said then blushed at why she wanted him to be healthy again: her wedding night.

Marty saw her blush then reflected it back to her. "Are we about done here, Nate? I have a wedding to plan!"

Nate looked at the half-empty IV bag and said, "I think you need to wait a few hours before you start off on your honeymoon. And, you might want to be healthy enough to eat a meal and walk across the room by yourself before you undertake, um, anything more strenuous. Now, I'll leave you three alone and see about getting you a clear meal. I take it you haven't eaten anything substantial in a while?"

Marty shook his head, remembering the small amount of ham he had eaten days before, the last gift Red Shirt had given him. "No, not for at least three days."

"Well, then, I'll give you a choice: red or green Jell-O?" Nate asked as he stood by the door, ready to retrieve his charge's meal.

"I'll go for the green. And bring some for everyone," Marty said playfully, realizing that this was just the first of many meals he would have with his 21st century, North Carolina family.

20 What next?

"Oh, my God," Marty exclaimed after Nate left the room, suddenly bringing the joyful mood of his family down to the ground.

"What's wrong?" Billy and Bibb chorused.

"My coin; I left it back at the site. I don't want someone to find it there. I mean, it's not the monetary value, but if someone finds it there, especially a child with an active imagination, or one of those Revolutionary War re-enactors, they could be flung back in time and not know what in the blazes happened. Good Lord, how could I have been so careless?" Marty moaned.

"Uh, you had other things on your mind, like staying alive. But, don't worry, Dad, I have it right here." Billy held up the silver Greek drachma with two holes drilled in it. "You don't want to use it again, do you?" Billy asked, his apprehension showing as his voice squeaked at the end of his question.

"No way, Jose! At least not unless you two want to go, too," Marty replied. He brought Bibb's hand up to his face. "It's a rough life, but if you want to go, I'll get another coin." He looked up at Billy. "And, one for you, too, son. I really, really don't want to be separated from you two ever again."

"Me either," Billy said. "Although, I hope you feel the same way after getting to know me better; me and my family that is…"

"I'm sure your father will love Peter just as much as I do," Bibb said proudly, showing her support for her son's alternative lifestyle.

"I'm sure I will," Marty said, glad that he had been forewarned by his other son, James, that Billy had a same-sex partner. Marty reached out to hold Billy's hand. "If he's good enough for you, son, then he's good enough for me, us, too."

"Oh, and Peter doesn't know anything about you and James being time traveling fairies," Billy joked. He then brought his perky tone down a notch. "But, there is another one of you out there," he said seriously.

Marty tried to bring the mood up again. "What, another fairy?" he asked lightly. He looked at Billy, then Bibb, and saw this was important—they were getting ready to lay a bomb on him.

"Did you ever read the *Lost* novels by Lisa Sinclaire?" Billy asked.

Marty nodded, saving his words. He was starting to tire but didn't want the two of them to feel obligated to leave. After he had read Evie's first letter years ago, he had waited for the first of the Lisa Sinclaire novels to be published, anxiously awaiting each episode to be released so he could find out more about the Pomeroys, the family 20th century-born Evie, the letter-writing, time traveling fairy, had married into during the Revolutionary War.

"Well, they're true, at least parts of the stories. You see, two months ago, just after James and Leah went back through The Trees to see you and her mother, Evie, someone came to me looking for Leah. It was Jody Pomeroy's grandson, Benji. He said he wanted to go back with her to the 18th century to see his grandparents; that he had been born then, came forward to the 20th century as a child, and grew up here in this time. Dad, they're real, the Pomeroys and MacKays; they're not fictional characters. Those are history books written by Lisa Sinclaire, not historical novels. Benji's here, now, but he's going back, too."

"Well," Marty said, "I met Benji when he was yay high, he and his father. But, I had no idea that they, or rather Benji, wanted to go back. And, I did get a chance to meet Jody's nephew Ian Kincaid when I was back there. He was, is, Bibb's great-great however so many times over, grandfather. He was the reason I went back. I thought you knew about that. Didn't James share the letters with you before he left?"

Billy and Bibb shook their heads in tandem, but it was Billy who spoke up. "They were stolen before James could read beyond the first one. It's a good thing he read it though, or Leah would never have known that her mother went back in time, was alive and well in 1781, and had another family. They're okay, aren't they, James and Leah, that is?"

"They took off in the opposite direction from me about two months ago. I'm sure they're fine. They had horses, food and water, and good directions," Marty explained, then remembered that they hadn't read the rest of the letters. Neither James nor Leah's arrival or life had been recorded in them, but he didn't want to tell them that. He could only hope they had sent their dialogues to a different place and they just hadn't been found yet.

"So tell me more about this other fairy, Benji," Marty said then looked to his IV bag. "He's bound to have changed a bit in the last twenty years and I need some distraction while I'm waiting to get a refill."

End of Book Three

Preview of the fourth in the series, THE GREAT BIG FAIRY, follows.

Preview of THE GREAT BIG FAIRY:

"Well, Dad," Billy said with a big inhale, proud of having a father, a living father, who he could use that designation with, "this is how it went down a few months ago. Actually, I remember the date: August 17, 2013. Let me tell you the story like a narrator. I'm still pretty tender about their loss—I mean James and Leah leaving. But, you need to know what was going on in my head when I met him, Benji, the biggest, sweetest man there ever was."

Billy began his narration sounding just like Dan Akroyd in *Dragnet* then quickly segued into his own voice:

"Greensboro, North Carolina, Police Department. Billy was finally finished with his paperwork. It had been a long night. James and Leah had left only an hour and a half ago and, unless something drastic occurred, and he didn't even want to speculate on that possibility, he would never see his newfound brother or sister-in-law/best friend again. But, now he, Billy Burke, the lifelong orphan, had a mother, and that blessing he had stopped hoping for about fifteen years ago. He also knew who his father was and, although he may never be able to meet the elusive Marty Melbourne, he could find out more about him from his mother, the sweetest woman in the world, Bibb Stephens.

"There was no reason for him to delay his final task. It was time to head out of town and pick up his going away present from James—the 'Beast', the classic 1964 red Dodge pickup truck. He would get one of the officers to drop him off near the site. He wouldn't have to give him an explanation. That would make the task easier, but he still wasn't ready to admit the finality of their departure. He missed them both already and actually hurt physically from their absence. The ache of emptiness went from his shoulders to his kneecaps and made it feel like his spine was an iced up rope, just dangling down through his midsection, holding his pelvis to his collarbones. He snorted; Leah would have told him that that was anatomically impossible, but that *was* how he felt.

"He gathered up the piles of reports, straightened the edges by banging them just a little too hard on the top of the desk, and tugged at the drawer with more force than necessary. It felt like his left hand had four thumbs as he fumbled through the dividers. He finally found the file for the case and tossed it in like a shovelful of coal into a furnace, messing up the neat pile he had just put it in. "That's enough of you!" he said. Hopefully, he would never hear the name Atholl MacLeod again.

"Sir, there's someone here to see you. He says it's very important," Dyane called on the intercom.

"Have Sergeant Carter take care of it, will you? I'm off shift now," he replied with exasperation. He realized it was the wrong tone but it was better than the one he was holding back. He didn't know if he wanted to scream, or cry, or laugh. But, he did know that this was not the place to let loose. He stood up to leave then scanned the remaining papers still on his desk, making sure they were devoid of anything that would remind him of his time traveling family when he came back to work that evening.

"Sir," Dyane came back, "He says it's about someone named Evie and her daughter, Leah, the nurse. He says you'll know who he's talking about."

"Billy went weak in the knees then everywhere else. Fortunately, his chair was strategically placed, catching him as he plopped down solidly in a controlled fall. He swallowed hard, started to speak, but only an embarrassing squeak came out. He tried again. "Send him in," he said, this time, the words coming together and finding a way out of his mouth.

198

"Dyane opened the door for the large visitor. Billy stood up and his eyes widened as they watched the man duck his head in order to enter his office. He wasn't the tallest man he had ever seen; he had met a couple of the gangly basketball players with the Hornets, but he was the biggest in terms of being a proportionately built man. Billy quickly tipped his head down when he realized he was staring. He walked around to the front of his desk to shake the hand of the huge man with auburn red hair. He glanced up again and the gentle giant grinned and whispered, "Six seven," like he was sharing a secret.

"Billy pointed to the chair, offering his congenial new acquaintance a place to sit, then walked back around his desk, touching its surface as much for reassurance that he was awake as for physical support, lest he fall down from shock. He sat down slowly in his seat, his head bowed down, concentrating on the desktop. He didn't think he could make the transition from standing to sitting while looking into the face of this big man.

"I didn't mean to stare," Billy apologized as he looked up again. "It's just that you remind me of someone. All you're missing is the Scots accent." Billy couldn't help but think of the man's resemblance to Jody Pomeroy of the *Lost* novels. If James and Leah had just gone back to his time, the 18th century,could it be that Jody Pomeroy had come back here, to this time? He fought back the urge to shake his head 'no' in answer to his own unspoken question and smiled nervously.

"Weel, I guess I lost a bit of the accent since I've been back here in North Carolina. Now, that bein' said, are ye the one to talk to about Leah and Evie?"

"Who *are* you?" Billy asked incredulously before he answered the Jody look-alike's question.

"I'm sorry. I dinna introduce myself. I'm Benjamin MacKay, but ye can call me Benji."

"Billy nodded his head slowly in answer to Benji's question about being familiar with Leah and Evie. He didn't even try to talk lest the sounds come out as the 'baa, baa, babble' that were coursing through his brain. He'd read all the Lisa Sinclaire novels at least once. Benji was Jody Pomeroy's grandson, and he was now sitting in front of him, all grown up. He was supposed to be a fictional character!

"Weel then, I hope it's not too late to catch a ride back with Leah. I got distracted with a couple of unsavory characters. But, it seems that ye've helped me quite a bit and have the MacLeod brothers out of my hair now. I, um, *heard* that Leah was goin' *back* to see her mother soon. I understand she knows how to, um, *travel* safely and without a lot of pain involved?" he asked rather than stated, focusing on Billy's eyes for his reaction.

"Benji could see by the detective's wide-eyed and slack-jawed appearance that Billy understood what he was talking about. He waited for Billy's reply, but the stunned police officer just sat at his desk, palms flat like he was holding down the wooden furniture down, and shook his head back and forth slowly. "You're too late," he whispered, his head still moving back and forth at the same, slow pace. "About two hours too late. They've already gone."

"Benji winched, shut his eyes, and shook his head with a look of sadness and frustration. "Jest two hours..." he exhaled. "Um, do ye happen to know how they traveled?" he asked tentatively.

"Billy pinched the bridge of his nose and rubbed his thumb and index finger out over his eyebrows, rubbing them back and forth in a nervous manner. He wanted to delay the answer. He didn't know if this Benji, this 21st century Benji, was a good person or not. Could it be that he was in with the MacLeods? But, before he answered, he heard the cautious question.

"Are ye related to Marty Melbourne, per chance?"

"Billy's head snapped to attention, the fog of indecision blown away with the hurricane force of the shocking inquiry. "Why?" was all that he could think to answer.

"Benji chortled. "Weel, ye must be then or ye woulda answered 'who' or 'no.' Ye look jest like him, have his same nervous habit of pinchin' yer eyebrows, and I'll wager if ye had the English accent, ye'd sound jest like him, too. But, yer not James, are ye? I mean, yer an American and an officer of the law. He's a member of parliament and a businessman."

"Billy drew a deep breath, making the snap, gut decision that this was a good man and could be trusted. "James is my brother and Marty is my father," he said with a big exhale. He started to say more of their relationship but stopped. He'd let Benji talk and see how much he knew.

"Ye said 'they' went back, not jest Leah. Who went with her?" Benji asked.

"James did. He's her husband now. I don't think he would have let her go by herself. He was quite smitten with her. They only knew each other two weeks, but as soon as I saw those two together, I knew that it wouldn't be too long and... Hey, how did you know Leah went back?" Billy asked, losing his original train of thought. This man was sharp and didn't miss a word.

"I read about it in a letter," Benji said plainly. He opened his mouth to say more then decided he'd wait to see if this American was going to let something slip. He wanted to know how much he knew before talking about time travel to a total stranger.

"But Billy was smart, too. He was also playing the 'show me your cards and I'll show you mine' game. "So how do you know Marty Melbourne?" he asked with a glint in his eye, letting the big Scot know they were playing mental poker.

"Benji grinned and replied, "Ye make a livin' out of this, aye? I mean, jest any little thing a man says, ye can use to find out more about a situation."

"Billy pointed to the first part of the nametag on his desk. "It says detective, aye? So how do ye ken him?" he asked, mimicking Benji's accent.

"He came to our place when I was much younger. He and my father talked fer quite a while. Ye see, my father had read a letter about a James Melbourne and was tryin' to find him. He dinna ken much about him or his family, but what he kent was enough. It turns out that both men were lookin' fer each other. My father was writin' a book about, um, writin' a book that interested Lord Melbourne, and the two actually took a trip here to North Carolina in the early 90's. Young James and I came with them."

"Billy decided to lay out a card and see if he could gain Benji's confidence. "So was the book about," he paused then made eye contact with the large red haired man, "about time travel?"

"What?" his new acquaintance laughed, "Do ye believe in that nonsense?"

"But, Billy could tell that Benji was just having fun with him. The walls were down and they were now both comfortable. "So, does this mean that you've traveled and it was painful? I mean, you mentioned Leah finding a way to travel without pain."

"Benji rolled his eyes. "Ye have no idea how painful. I was jest a lad, but I get the cold goose flesh jest thinkin' about it. I guess this means ye never went, um, back?"

"No, I'm sort of new to all of this. Have you had breakfast yet? I'm just getting off work and I think we have a lot to talk about."

"And that's how we met," Billy told Marty. "But there's so much more to the story. Stick around and I'll tell you about it."

End of Preview of THE GREAT BIG FAIRY ~ Fourth in the
series THE FAIRIES SAGA

Visit: www.danihaviland.com
For previews of other books in the series

Thanks to my husband, Marty, and youngest daughter, Bibb, for being patient and supportive in my writing efforts and not getting upset that I 'borrowed' their names for my characters.

Thanks to youngest brother, Tony Woodward, for the beautiful painting, 'Lost in the Wilderness,' that I used for the book cover. As soon as I saw it, I knew where it belonged.

Thanks to my editor and the best body worker / healer in the world, Cathie Woods, for her creative and grammatical suggestions, many of which I used. She has been enthusiastic about my efforts and made sure she let me know the positive, healthy effects creative channeling has had on my (getting to be an) old lady body. Maybe if I write more, *I'll* get younger…

A grateful nod to James Pietz, a guy who fell short of his dream of being the village idiot, but during a lucid interval stumbled upon a fix to a technical annoyance I was having with my documents.

Thank you, America and our valiant protectors, for securing my freedom of speech along with so many other rights and privileges still promised in our Bill of Rights. Because of them, I can share my wandering, imaginative mind without fear of repercussions. I have fun, fearlessly time tripping, knowing that there *really* is a way to travel in time; it's just that we haven't discovered how to put the science and hardware together.

Then again, the secret of time travel may already be known by a select few. I know *if* I knew how to bounce back and forth between the centuries, I'd keep it to myself, too (grin).

And remember—always be nice to one another,

Dani Haviland

www.danihaviland.com

www.ingramcontent.com/pod-product-compliance
Lightning Source LLC
Chambersburg PA
CBHW031332170626
46807CB00002B/665